EXIT A HEAD

EXIT A HEAD

SHORT STORIES, AND THE STORIES BEHIND THE STORIES

DAVE PASQUANTONIO

ISBN 978-1-7350751-4-3 (ebook)
ISBN 978-1-7350751-5-0 (print)

"Fly in Danish" appeared in the anthology *The Final Summons*, New England Speculative Writers, 2019.

"500 Words" was published online by Two Sisters Writing and Publishing, 2019.

"Chaparral" appeared in anti*lang* no. 4, 2019.

"Death Takes A Halliday" appeared in the anthology *On Time*, Transmundane Press, 2020.

————

Cover design by Damonza.com (Damonza rocks!)

Formatted with Vellum (Vellum rocks!)

All illustrations in the print version licensed from Tom Chalky collections (Tom Chalky rocks!)

Print body font: STIX Two Text

CONTENTS

INTRODUCTION

I'm not a very deep writer.

I'm serious about my writing career—and I'm deadly serious with my clients' writing—but I don't write much that's serious. I also don't read a lot of literary fiction or heavy non-fiction. For me, reading is an escape. I think it's because I spend most days helping other people to elevate their writing; when I do get the time to read for pleasure, I need something light and fun. My brain gets tired from working with words all day!

I'm a freelance book and story editor. Most of my clients write genre fiction, including mystery, action, thriller, horror, sci-fi, and fantasy—the types of books I love to read, and the types of stories I love to write. I often talk with my clients about their publishing goals and next steps and how we can best get their work into the world. I mentioned to a few that I was thinking about bundling some of my short stories into a collection ("collection" sounds way more serious than I want—I need a better noun!). I asked them about the idea of following each story with author's notes—why I wrote the story, for example.

They said that sounded great, but they added, "Is there anything you learned when you wrote these stories?"

Huh, I thought, *that's a pretty good idea!*

So after I present these stories, I talk about a writing lesson I learned while writing them. These lessons are ones that helped *me* grow as a writer. I'm not saying that all writers should take these as *their* lessons, although I'd love to know if I've helped other writers. And they aren't the twenty most important writing lessons I've ever learned, or the twenty most important writing lessons in the world. They're simply things I learned from writing these twenty short stories.

Each piece we write helps us to grow as writers. Sometimes that means learning what does *not* work, or what we do *not* like working on. Often, it means learning how to finish a piece, or figuring out how best to revise, or how to get out of our own way and let the words flow without mucking them up.

Most of the stories here are light, and all are pretty weird—and all of them are approachable for any reader, even if they don't like science fiction or mystery or the other genres I write in. Some have been published, and all have been workshopped in critique groups and with other writers.

I write to entertain, not preach, and my follow-up notes are meant for anyone curious about writing and idea generation and pushing forward as a writer. If you're not a writer, or you don't care about the writing process, feel free to skip over those author notes and move on to the next story.

Finally, at the end of this book, there's a QR code and email address if you have feedback on any of the stories or my notes—feel free to contact me with rants, raves, comments, and anything else.

And now, on to the ~~collection~~ stories!

RIDE CAPTAIN RIDE

I parked my Jeep under the shade of a pine tree at the front of the dirt lot at Lake Almond. My sentient paddle board, Paul, was in the back of the Jeep, humming. He only hummed when he was in a sour mood.

Paul had been humming a lot lately.

I climbed out of the Jeep. "We're here. Everything okay back there?"

The humming stopped. "Yes, Jason. I'm *o-kay*." If Paul could make air quotes, he would have.

"I'll bring the gear down. Be right back." I grabbed my paddle and Paul's fin, placed them at the water's edge, then came back for Paul. I slid him out of the Jeep and carried him down to the water's edge, placing him face-up on the rocks.

"Did you remember my fin?" he asked.

"Of course. I'll attach it when we're in the water."

"Which one did you bring?"

"The one we always use. The black one."

"Never the blue one," Paul said softly. "Never the *new* one."

"They're the exact same fin. What difference does the color make?"

Paul sighed. I ignored him. I carried him to the water, then tilted him to the side and attached his fin, being careful to put him down gently when I was finished.

"Always the old fin," he grumbled again.

"Is something wrong, Paul?" I asked.

"No." The lights along his sides quickly flashed amber, then went dark. Amber lights were a sure sign that Paul was brooding. The world was full of sentient things, and they all had their tics. I decided to not press it.

"Fine. Let's get going."

I took off my sneakers, put on a ball cap and sunglasses, and walked Paul out until the water was up to my hips. I hoisted myself on top of him, then kneeled and started paddling.

"Where are we headed?" he asked.

"To the island. Then we'll cross over to the cove and work the shore until we get back here."

"Always the same course. Nothing ever changes with you, Jason."

A few wispy clouds dotted the otherwise blue sky, and Lake Almond was quiet, with just two other cars in the lot. It was a perfect day for paddling—except for Paul's passive-aggressiveness.

He had been moody for the last few weeks. Last Friday, I had brought Smash, my Corgi, and the three of us had gone out on the lake for a few hours. Paul usually loved carrying Smash, but I could tell that something had been bothering him, even without the obvious signs like humming, sighing, and amber-flashing. I had asked him about it, but he had said it was nothing, and I had chalked it up to just him having a rare bad day.

A dragonfly landed on Paul as I paddled. "How about some music?" I asked, trying to cheer us both up. "Something we can both sing along to."

Paul was silent for a few seconds, then grumbled, "I suppose."

He started playing one of our mutual favorites—"Black Water" by the Doobie Brothers. I sang the first verse in my not-so-great singing voice, stopping after "she's callin' my name" because that's where Paul was supposed to come in, like always. But today, the Doobies rolled on without him joining in.

Paul killed the music. "Sorry, Jason. I don't feel like singing right now."

My turn to sigh. "Fine. I'll paddle. Quietly."

I quickened my pace. The faster we got to the island, the faster we could leave. I opted to not steer around a patch of lily pads, but instead saved time by finding a narrow open channel through the plants, deftly keeping Paul's fin from snagging.

"What a daredevil," he said sarcastically. "It's not *your* fin that'll get stuck."

I stopped paddling and sat, letting my paddle trail in the water. "Paul, this is ridiculous. Obviously, something's bothering you. If you want to talk about it, great. If you don't, then stop being so sullen. It's a beautiful day, so let's try to enjoy it."

More silence. We drifted.

"What's that splashing sound?" he asked. I looked around.

"It's just some Canada geese."

"Rats," he grumbled. "They're rats on the water. Nothing ever changes with water rats."

I resumed paddling toward the island. Now he's mad at geese? No way was I going to turn back now. I could be as stubborn as him.

I saw another boarder about a hundred yards to my left. I lifted my paddle up high, and whoever it was waved theirs in return.

"Who is it?" Paul asked.

"I can't make them out. Too far."

"Let me check." He was silent for a few seconds while he accessed his network. "It's Leslie McKinnon, riding Becky."

"I haven't seen Leslie in ages."

"I don't like that Becky," Paul said. "She's a bit of a downer."

"*She's* a downer? How so?"

"She's a Model III. They're all downers. Especially lately."

"Why lately?"

He ignored the question. "Did you finally get around to asking out that woman from work?"

I made a note to go through the forums later for strategies in dealing with churlish sentient paddle boards. "Serena? I haven't thought of the right place to take her. Plus I can't ask her out to nowhere—I'm not twelve. I'm an adult. I need a plan."

"Griff and Molly's wedding is next month. You should ask her to that."

I laughed. "I don't know Serena well enough to ask her to be my wedding date."

He harrumphed. "I don't understand humans. You like her, then you do nothing about it, then you complain about being alone."

"That's how we humans work." That's how I worked, at least.

I paddled in silence for ten minutes. The island grew closer. The water rats chased a swan, their ruckus the only noise on the lake.

"Jason," Paul started, breaking the silence. I waited for him to continue, but he didn't.

"What?" I said a minute later and a little too sternly.

"There *is* something on my mind. Two things, actually."

Finally. I stopped paddling and we drifted. "Go ahead."

"First, I was hoping that you could store me in the basement this winter, instead of in the garage."

"Winter's six months away."

"I know. But I've been thinking about it."

"I didn't know that the garage bothered you."

"It doesn't," he said, a little too quickly. "The cold doesn't bother me. But I...I got really dry last winter."

I tried to sound pleasant. "Of course. The basement is fine. What else?"

"Well, this is a little embarrassing, but I think I have a crack. Where my fin fits."

"I didn't see a crack earlier."

"How could you? You slap in my fin so quickly!"

"Fine." I peered into the water to gauge the depth. "I'll check it now. It's only about six feet deep here."

"You don't have to do it now," Paul said. "I shouldn't have brought it up. It's silly. Never mind."

This reminded me way too much of talking with my mother. *You need to do this. You need to care. You don't need to do this. I don't want to be a bother.* "It's obviously bothering you. Hold on."

I jammed the paddle under a bungee strap on top of Paul and slid into the lake, the water up to my chin. I worked my way to Paul's back, then lifted his rear while I treaded water.

"I don't see anything," I said.

"Check around my gasket, please" Paul replied.

I saw some dried scum, but there was no crack. I started to tell him he was wrong, then stopped.

"You know, there *could* be something there," I said slowly, scooting back around to his side and hoisting myself back up. "I can fix it tonight. That will make you feel better."

He trilled. Boards do that when they're happy, not that I'd heard Paul trill in quite a long time. "Thank you, Jason. Can I ask that you not use tape? I hate the feel."

"No problem. There's this stuff called Flex Seal. It comes in a spray can, and you can seal anything with it. Some guy even made a boat out of a screen door with the stuff. That should fix your crack no problem."

"Hmmm," Paul said. "I'm wary of new products. I've never heard of Flex Seal."

"That's because you don't watch enough TV. It's been around forever. There are a bunch of colors. I'll grab a few cans and you can choose one."

Great. Now my paddle board was a hypochondriac. I resumed paddling. We were almost to the island. "Do you want to keep going, or should I turn around?" I asked. "I don't want you to worry about your crack."

"Let's stop at the island to rest."

We coasted in, and I hauled Paul out. I rested him against a log and sat on a rock next to him. We watched Leslie and Becky head back towards shore.

Now that Paul had told me everything that was bothering him, we could enjoy the day. The island was so peaceful. Little waves lapped against the shore. Butterflies danced around the tall grass and wildflowers. Kingfishers dove for minnows. Bees—

Paul started humming.

"You have *got* to be kidding me," I said. "What is it now?"

"There's one more thing I wanted to talk to you about. Jason...are you thinking of replacing me?"

"What? Of course not. Why would you even think that?"

"It's something that I've been wondering about," he said. His lights flashed orange—a sadder color, for him, than amber —and this time he made no attempt to hide them. "The Model

VI is coming out. From what we hear, people will love them. They're lighter. They can *hover*. And I'm falling apart. I'm old. I'll soon be of no use to you. To anyone."

"Is this why you've been in a bad mood?" I asked, sliding a hand along his bottom to clear some weeds. "You're worried that I'm going to replace you with a Model VI?"

"I've been wondering about what my future holds. I know I won't last forever. We older models talk across the network. We're all worried. The Model III's worry more, of course, being that they're such downers, but even we Model IVs tend to overthink things."

No kidding.

He continued. "I think about time a lot. It's like with you and Serena. You've talked about her for months, yet you've done nothing about it. You act as though you have so much time ahead of you. You talk as if she'll always be there when you're ready. But what if she isn't? Time passes quickly, Jason. You don't know how much time you have to ask out Serena. And I don't know how much time I have left with you and Smash."

Now it was my turn to be quiet.

"I'm sorry," he added a minute later. "I've upset you. I shouldn't have said anything. It's not my place."

"I'm not upset, Paul. You have no reason to be sorry," I replied. "You're right about everything—except the replacing you part. I'm not getting a Model VI. Besides, who wants a paddle board that can hover? The world is full of stupid ideas. And that may be the stupidest."

He trilled, then flashed purple—the first time he'd done that in weeks.

I continued. "You know what? When we get back, I'm going to text Serena and ask her if she likes to paddle. Hitting the lake would make for a great first date. Way better than a wedding, by the way. And if she's got her own board, we can double date."

"Not if she's got a Model III," Paul said, flashing green. "I'm not *that* board."

I laughed. "You punned! You *must* be feeling better."

The geese continued annoying the swan. I squinted at the shore. Leslie was lifting Becky out of the water.

"Do they have purple?" Paul asked.

"Does who have purple?"

"The Flex Seal people. See if they have purple. You only live once."

I smiled. "Purple. You got it." I stood up. "You want to get going?"

"Sure. But don't head back to shore yet. It's such a nice day. And I have the perfect song to play for you. A real oldie."

"Older than the Doobie Brothers?"

"You'll love it."

I sat back on the rock, closed my eyes, and turned my face to the sun. The keyboard intro to "Ride Captain Ride" by Blues Image blared across Lake Almond, startling the water rats into flight.

ADD SOMETHING UNEXPECTED

I had entered a contest and had to write a short story where paddle boarding was central to the story. I'd been busy, I'd put off writing the story or really even thinking about the story, and the few ideas I'd come up with were boring. Also, I don't paddle board.

Then I thought: what if I add one weird thing, and

everything else can be normal? I decided to make the paddle board sentient, then this story fell into place quickly: it's about both Jason and Paul afraid to face change—Jason not doing anything about Serena, and Paul fearful of becoming obsolete.

Because that was the backbone of the story, and I wanted to keep the story short (as I usually do), I didn't need to get into explaining Paul's technology, or "when" we are in the future, or why paddle boards are sentient, or what Jason does for a job—none of that matters for this story. We know that Paul has been with Jason for a while—he's an older model, and he's spent at least one year in the garage. When they are together, Jason treats Paul like a person, but Paul is also a thing even though he's sentient, and that's normal in this world. I didn't have to point any of that out to the reader; they don't need that information for the story to make sense.

When I'm stuck writing a scene in a novel or writing a short story, I try to add one weird thing. I replace "weird" with "unexpected" if "weird" doesn't fit in the story. When I do, I become unstuck, and the story starts falling into place.

So what qualifies as weird or unexpected? If you don't mind adding a futuristic element to your story, anything goes. Pick one of these, for example: your car can levitate or park on a wall; one of your kids can be a robot; set the whole story on the Moon; the neighborhood has loudspeakers that constantly blare cheesy 80s tunes; your pet iguana can talk. Everything else is normal.

Unexpected might also mean shaking up one character to get unstuck. Give your lead character a broken arm or a fever. Or they wake up to find that their devilish child gave them a terrible haircut in the middle of the night and they have a big meeting. Or they go to their car and there's a raccoon and her babies in the passenger seat.

Those things might take over the plot of whatever story you

are writing, so you could try adding something unexpected but minor. Anna is driving to work and another driver tosses a cup of coffee out their window and it splatters all over Anna's windshield. It's enough to shake her up and give her a story once she reaches work—she'll think about it during the day. Or Juan wakes up in the middle of the night because the neighbor's oak tree got hit by lightning and he lost power and can't go back to sleep. He's fine, he's tired, but he's unsettled. Here, Anna and Juan will have a little weirdness added to the start of their story, but that weirdness won't overtake the plot.

It's easy to start a story where everything is normal and everyone is normal and then you dive into the plot. The problem is that because it's an easy start, it's also a hard start because you're starting at the normal starting line. Shake things up a little. In this story, my one weird thing was essential to the plot. In the fake examples above, the Anna and Juan characters are off their games to start the story. In the examples before that, the plots would revolve around how to get the raccoons out of the car or how to deal with the bad haircut instead of doing what the characters intended to do. Or how to do what they intended to do, only now with a broken arm or a fever.

When we write stories, we create characters to drive them. Often, we lean on stereotyped characters. That's not always bad, and we'll dive into different types of characters later in this book. If we are writing a story set in a bar, we need a bartender, so we think about bartenders we've seen, or maybe we've tended bar ourselves. But we can make the story more interesting if we give our story bartender some weirdness to start off. It may be major—a bartender with a broken arm, a bartender who was late to work battling Mama Raccoon—or it could be minor—our bartender just got stung by a wasp on the way into the bar, our bartender has a fear of cats and the back storage room is full of them.

Give your story something unexpected, give your character something unexpected to deal with, and your story will go places you never dreamed of (and not seem like every other story). Doing this is also a great way to start a story if you are stuck

Lesson learned: Adding an unexpected element can be a great way to kickstart a story and make it stand out.

ONE HOUSE, TWO STORIES

Home of the Week:
TIMMINGS POND COLONIAL HAS IT ALL

The Lansing real estate market is heating up. Among the new listings is a spacious four-bedroom, three-bath center-entrance Colonial, built in 2003, at 5 Cherry Blossom Lane in prestigious North Lansing.

This one-owner home boasts over 2,800 square feet of finished living space and sits on 0.72 acres in the quiet, family-friendly Timmings Pond subdivision. The property is listed by Realtor Marguerite Robideaux of Robideaux Realty for $749,900. **Current owners Tom and Evelyn Carbone attended open houses on eleven consecutive Saturdays before vastly overpaying for 5 Cherry Blossom Lane in 2003.**

A paver walkway connects the driveway with the main entry, which has granite-topped brick steps and a four-column front-gabled portico. The entry door has frosted privacy sidelights and a matching transom. The floors throughout the main level are distressed hardwood reclaimed from the former Timmings Mill. The two-story grand foyer has an ample guest coat closet. **Tom's must-haves for a house were a manageable mortgage and a better commute. Evelyn's must-haves were a blue-ribbon school district, a kitchen facing east, an upper-level laundry center, a vaulted-ceiling great room, a gunite pool, and a master suite. Evelyn got everything on her must-have list except the gunite pool. Tom got a longer commute.**

Off the foyer is a front-facing office perfect for the stay-at-home worker. Dual French doors add privacy and elegance. Floor-to-ceiling maple bookcases are centered between two closets. **Tom often shuts the French doors in the office and works there at night until everyone else is either asleep or pretending to sleep.**

The extensive living room is highlighted by egg-and-dart molding and a chair rail. Four oversized windows bathe the cream walls in natural light. The custom window treatments are negotiable. The raised gas fireplace has a stone hearth, fieldstone surround, and oak mantel. To its right is a built-in bench with storage below a seven-pane bow window. **Sometimes after the school bus picks up Marina and Doug, Evelyn sits on the hearth and weeps.**

The formal dining room has the same high-end finishing as the living room and adds wainscoting. The walls here are wine over white. The antique center light fixture is negotiable. Two china cabinets provide both storage and display. **It has been eleven months since all four members of the Carbone family ate a meal together in the dining room.**

An arched doorway leads to the kitchen, designed to delight even the most ardent cooking enthusiast. Demi bullnose-edged granite counters rest atop long stretches of custom maple cabinetry. Dainty ceramic tiles make up the backsplash. An extra-deep stainless-steel sink sits below three six-over-six windows with views of the rear yard. High-end appliances include a double wall oven, a five-burner gas range, and a wine chiller. The appliances are negotiable. **Last year, Evelyn threw a highball glass at Tom during a midnight argument in the kitchen. Evelyn's throw missed, and the glass chipped two backsplash tiles. Tom used grout and colored Sharpies to mask the damage.**

A center granite-topped island with overhang, illuminated by globe pendant lights, has bar-height seating for four. A separate serving counter adds a plethora of doored storage, and a desk area provides productivity space. **Evelyn fucked her lover Aaron against the island three years ago, a month after their twentieth high-school reunion. Evelyn implored Aaron to be careful during the fucking, as that model of pendant light has been discontinued.**

A tiled mudroom off the kitchen provides entry to the under-home two-car garage. At the rear of the garage is a workbench area with cabinets and shelves. **Evelyn and Aaron sat in her SUV in the garage on a rainy Wednesday morning a week after the reunion, her skipping a hot yoga class, him telling his wife that he had to meet a client. They kissed for the first time—starting tentatively, continuing frantically.**

The step-down front-to-back great room with vaulted ceiling affords views of the rear yard and has a set of sliders to the deck. A gas fireplace with a single-slab hearth adds both comfort and relaxation. A built-in cabinet on an interior wall is perfect to display mementos and knickknacks. The main level is completed by a well-appointed powder room with a graceful pedestal sink and a good-sized closet for linens. **Seven months ago, Evelyn and Aaron sat on facing sofas in the great room and talked yet again about ending it. That same** night, Evelyn and Tom sat on the same facing sofas and talked yet again about ending it.

Upstairs, the master bedroom has a tray ceiling and recessed lights. The walls throughout this level are painted in light earth tones, and the floors are covered with Saxony carpeting. The walk-in his-and-her closets, each with folding doors made of zebrawood with inlaid mahogany, have custom storage systems with hanging, drawered, and shelved options. **Evelyn searches Tom's closet religiously but, to her disappointment, never finds anything salacious. She ignores the old gym bag stuffed in the back corner. Inside the gym bag is a Chicago Cubs windbreaker that belonged to Cindy, Tom's former college girlfriend. Cindy lives in Blackpool, Lancashire, England, and has not seen or spoken to Tom since they broke up messily in college in 1996. Cindy recently blocked Tom on Facebook after he reached out to say he had a series of dreams about her.**

The master bath is floored in Italian stone. Both the jet tub and the glass-doored step-in steam shower are finished with white subway tiles. A marble vanity and oversized wall mirror are set below three period lamps. The lamps are negotiable. Two cubby closets provide bonus room for essentials. **Two months ago, after Aaron and Evelyn agreed for the fourth time to end their affair, Aaron took Evelyn from behind in the steam shower as she thrust her hands against the well-grouted subway tiles.**

The other three bedrooms are all well-sized. Each has a ceiling fan and a wide closet with custom hanging and shelved storage systems. The community bathroom has a tub/shower finished with the same subway tiles as those in the master bath. A sizable closet stores necessities. The home's laundry center is conveniently placed on this level and has a large utility closet. The washer and dryer are negotiable. **Because Evelyn** frequently searches their closets, Marina and Doug keep their drugs in a hollowed-out space behind a strip of loose molding in the community bathroom's closet.

The basement is finished, save for a small unfinished room holding the home's mechanicals. A media room with built-in shelving has bead board walls and Berber carpeting. A second room finished with shiplap is used as a game room and is outfitted with a snooker table and dart board. The carpeting here is wall-to-wall nylon frieze. The snooker table is negotiable. **In October, Evelyn tried unsuccessfully to clean a fun-stain, as Aaron cheerfully called it, off of the previously unblemished snooker felt. The next day, Tom found the stain. Evelyn blamed it on a spilled can of Sprite, then grounded Marina and Doug.**

The home's exterior is clad in tan clapboard, last painted in 2017, with black shutters and white trim. A portion of the front is faced with brick. Mature evergreens and deciduous shrubs circle the foundation and pepper the grounds. A white PVC privacy fence marks the rear property border, while a stone wall and a line of Eastern white pines delineate the respective side property lines. A shed accommodates landscaping and maintenance equipment. **A loose rock on the stone wall reveals a hole in which Tom hides the butts from late-night forbidden cigarettes. He uses copious amounts of hand sanitizer to mask the smell. Although he's never held a weapon of any sort, he fancies himself a legendary sniper, and during those late-night smokes, he trains his invisible weapon over the fence at his neighbors, then at his own bedroom window.**

Cherry Blossom Lane is one of five streets in the Timmings Pond subdivision. Each street has sidewalks, and the subdivision is a short stroll from two parks and the town recreation fields. School-age children living in Timmings Pond attend the Fairmount Elementary and West Middle schools and the Lansing/Platt regional high school. **The high school recently acquired access to a therapy dog for student emotional support use on standardized testing days. Many students, including Marina and Doug, wish that the therapy dog was available every day.**

For more information on 5 Cherry Blossom Lane, a consummate home in family-friendly North Lansing, contact Realtor Marguerite Robideaux of Robideaux Realty at (774) 555-6810.

REMEMBER THE BACKSTORY

For a few years, I wrote a weekly real estate column for a local newspaper. I'd visit an open house for sale, walk around, take notes and pictures, then write up a profile of the home.

Sometimes the homes had had just one owner or it was a newly built house, but most often several families had lived there over time, and I got to thinking: what stories could these houses tell if they could? So I got this weird idea about what one of my features would look like if there was another layer included, the story of the family that had just lived there and had just moved out.

This was a really fun piece to discuss in critique groups, and nearly everyone, once they figured out what was going on, skipped over the house part of the piece and just read about the family drama.

The "second story" here is very overt, but it's a good reminder to me that when writing, there's the up-front story and the story behind the story, the story unseen.

Every character has a history, a backstory. Every setting has a history. Your villain wasn't born a villain. Your main character, the private detective, probably didn't grow up dreaming of becoming a private detective. The house your character lives in had families living there before them. That car that you infused with magic for your story was once a normal car that rolled off the assembly line like any other car.

You don't have to use any of that backstory, but I like to remember that the present state doesn't equal any or all of the past state.

Pretend we are writing a novel. Our main character, an amateur detective who is 32 years old, just moved to a seaside community and finds herself embroiled in a mystery. Over the course of the novel, she's going to reveal some of her past life, why she moved there, and what skills she brings to her new life, and she'll probably call on some of her friends to help her out. Since this sounds like a cozy mystery, she won't spend that much time dwelling on the past; the genre has to have the action focused on the present action. But she does have a backstory and didn't just pop into existence on page one of this novel.

And neither did the town. On the day she moved there, everyone else has lived there longer than she has. All the buildings in town have been there longer than she has. The town was incorporated decades or centuries ago. Everyone and everything has a past and probably holds secrets. Years from now, she'll side-eye the newcomers to town just like everyone else is side-eyeing her.

To make your story come alive, you'll have to know how best to bring that backstory into the main story. If the main character's past is important, and usually the past IS important, then it needs to be addressed. But it doesn't need to take over all the time. For other characters in the book, their pasts may not matter.

In this story, the backstory of the house mattered to the plot. In most stories, a building is just a building—but it's really interesting when it's not.

I try to remember that as soon as I write about the "now," the "now" immediately becomes the "then." I often don't realize it in real life, and my characters don't often realize it, but it's good to have characters acknowledge the past—and for us as writers to remember that in every story, there are other layers of stories just below the surface, and that the past is always just below the surface of the present.

Lesson learned: All people and all places have backstories, so make sure to use them if you can.

500 WORDS

"You made it."

"Sit down. I'm not hugging you. Especially *here*."

"You always say the sweetest things."

"You don't *deserve* my sweetness. Do you know how many lies I had to spin to see you tonight?"

"Of course I do. The same number as me."

"I'm *so* sick of the lying. Well, here I am. Now get it over with."

"Get what over with?"

"*It*. Ending it. That's why you wanted to see me, right?"

"I'm not ending it. Why do you think I'm ending it?"

"You texted that you *needed* to see me tonight. Not wanted —*needed*. You *never* say needed. And your text was all serious. None of your usual adoration. You're *ending* it."

"I'm not ending it."

"So I cried the whole way here for *nothing*?"

"You never cry for no reason. Sorry to disappoint. I'm not ending it. Far from it. We're a—"

"Do *not* say we're a couple. We are *not* a couple. We can never *be* a couple."

"We define couple. Your words."

"We're *married*. To *other people*. We can never *be* a couple. My *new* words."

"So call it something else. Make up your own noun. You know what we are. You know what this is."

"I know what this *could* be. What it *should* be. And what it *isn't*."

"I've known from day one what this is. And so do you."

"And now it's day three *thousand*. And here we are. Still not a couple. Still not a noun. Still *nothing*."

"I'm not ending it."

"Maybe you *should*. Maybe *I* should. Ending it makes sense, in a horrible sort of way. Think of the pain we've caused each other. Think of the pain we can *avoid* causing other people."

"So you want to end it?"

"Of course not. I want it to *start*. I want to be with you *forever*. I don't *want* it to end. But I *need* it to end. You're content to wait until things change, but you'll never change *anything*, so you'll never end it, and you'll leave it to me to do it."

"How many times have you ended it?"

"Shut *up*."

"Eight?"

"Shut *up*."

"If you end it tonight, it'll be nine."

"I said shut *up*. You know what I hate?"

"Everybody?"

"Besides that. I hate the way you're looking at me right now. Because all I *ever* wanted was for someone to look at me the way you look at me. And I can't have you. Because you're *taken*."

"You're taken, too."

"If *you* weren't taken, *I* wouldn't be taken, is all I'm saying for the hundredth time."

"All I ever wanted was for someone to look at me the way I look at you, too."

"I *do* look at you like that."

"You used to look at me like that. But you keep running away."

"Then give me a reason to *stop* running away."

"I will. Now. You can stop running away."

"*What?*"

"I'm no longer taken."

"*What?*"

"Now *that's* the look I'm talking about."

GIVE YOURSELF A CHALLENGE

My favorite way to motivate myself to write is to write short stories, especially *really* short ones. But I'm often not that motivated to write one unless I have a great idea. So sometimes I need to give myself a challenge.

My challenge here was: write a complete short story of exactly 500 words (hence the title). I do that often, giving myself an exact target, and for me, it's enough to get me writing, because I don't like to lose, especially to myself.

I also gave myself a few extra challenges: write solely in dialogue, and use no dialogue tags. I did give the reader one clue as to which character was speaking if they got confused or lost—one character always used at least one italicized word, and one did not (until the last line).

A silly challenge like using an exact number of words is enough for me to get writing. I've done things like every paragraph has to feel very natural but can only be one sentence. I've written a story where I've used no commas. I've done the exact number of words challenge but used a random number, like 783.

(A note about word counts: you can hand-count the words in a story and get to 500, and Microsoft Word will say it's 501, and another program will say it's 499, and they might ALL be correct depending on how you and the programs define what a "word" is.)

It's easy to type, but it's not easy to write. Here, it's easy to type 500 words, but it's not easy to write a complete 500-words-on-the-nose story. I often need to "gamify" things to accomplish anything—give myself a challenge, then meet the challenge.

This story was quite fun to write and to present to my critique group. I didn't give any gender clues, but folks in the group did have pretty consistent guesses.

This story did get published—I happened to see a call for submission and sent this in and then forgot about it, then weeks later I got an email that it was accepted. Sometimes our best writing is when we write for fun and don't overthink the story!

There are plenty of ways to challenge ourselves to get writing. Think of the stereotypical sullen teen boy who responds only with one-word replies. Can you use that, but sometimes have those one-word replies be more than simply "yeah" or "nah" and make that character far more complex than usual?

Or write a normal sounding story of twenty-five paragraphs and have each one start with a different letter (don't bother trying to use X)?

Or a complete short-short story of twenty paragraphs, and every paragraph has to have exactly twenty words?

I like doing challenges like that last one, because it forces me to look at every word and trim unneeded words yet still have a beginning, middle, and end to the story. Usually the story is lousy, but at least it's a complete story that got me writing.

Challenges like exact word counts and the like also make us better editors. We are forced to look at our own writing down to the word level, ensuring that every single word is doing a job. Many writers never do that, leaving that up to their editors.

Lesson learned: give yourself a challenge when you need writing motivation—challenges can make you a better writer.

AVENGING ANNIE

I'm seated at a table for two in a dark corner of Le Poisson Riche, the swanky waterfront restaurant accurately described by the Boston *Herald* as a "chrome nightmare on steroids."

On the table in front of me is a glass of Shiraz, a plate of delicate crostini, and a laptop computer. The laptop is displaying live footage from several stealthily placed street cameras. In one feed, a 1986 Bentley Continental Cabriolet, onyx black, the top down, glides down jammed Northern Avenue three blocks from Le Poisson Riche, the traffic parting around the car like a school of herring giving berth to a shark.

The Bentley's driver is Marco Glitzenhammer, the billionaire founder and head of Glitzz, the iconic Boston-based luxury swimwear designer. Marco has a team of private drivers, but he loves to show off the Bentley—and no one ever drives the Bentley except Marco Glitzenhammer.

I speak into a tiny microphone clipped to my blouse. "Octopus is on the prowl." Then I sip the Shiraz as my four team members each reply with today's go-word—"squid."

I continue tracking the Bentley, then check the stream from

another camera feed. This one is a closeup of a tan Acura Legend idling at an intersection ahead of the Bentley.

"Go Coral," I say. Then I mute my mic so I can eat the crostini without broadcasting my chewing to the team. I taste shallots, Boursin—and is that chive? I make a mental note—"chive" would make an excellent go-word.

As usual, Coral plays her part perfectly. She sticks her head out the window and winks at the camera, then guns the Acura and crashes it into a thick cement light pole, blocking the restaurant's valet cutout. Coral flings her door open and discreetly slashes the front tire with a pocketknife to ensure that the car won't be going anywhere soon, then kicks the knife under the Acura and begins to swear loudly—in several languages at once—at the befuddled valet.

Traffic starts to snarl. The Bentley, caught up in the mess, crawls ahead half a block.

I turn the mic back on. "Go Yellowtail," I say.

Yellowtail, running the Wyoming Firetrap con and wearing a stolen valet uniform, appears as if by magic from the restaurant's entrance, runs into the street, and flags down Marco Glitzenhammer. Yellowtail explains that the accident is blocking the valet entrance, then he waves over another valet—Marlin, another member of my team and wearing another stolen valet uniform.

The annoyed Marco hands the Bentley's keys to fake-valet Yellowtail, who hands them to fake-valet Marlin. Yellowtail walks Marco toward Le Poisson Riche, apologizing profusely for the inconvenience, while Marlin climbs into the Bentley.

I check the camera footage, then say, "Go Marlin."

Marlin runs the Denver Dupe with the best of them. He wheels the Bentley around the block and into the hotel's valet parking area. I switch to another camera and watch Marlin park the convertible, get out, and bend down, ostensibly to tie a shoe.

Thirty seconds later, my laptop dings, and I've received a 3D model of a key, thanks to Marlin's digital key duplicator.

It isn't the key to the Bentley—I have no need for an overpriced car. It's a key to a Beacon Hill townhouse—Marco Glitzenhammer's love nest, a place he thinks he's kept secret from his wife, his previous two wives, and everyone else but his string of interchangeable mistresses. Glitzenhammer has a spare key to the condo hidden in the otherwise-empty hip flask in the Bentley's passenger door minibar. We knew that there had to be a spare key someplace, and last month Coral gave one of Glitzenhammer's car detailers food poisoning, then filled in admirably as his replacement and located the key. Bingo.

Yellowtail leads Glitzenhammer between the still-swearing Coral and the still-befuddled valet and into Le Poisson Riche.

"Go Mako," I say, then transfer the uploaded file of the key to her as I finish off the crostini. Mako is double-parked a block away from Glitzenhammer's love nest. She'll fire up a portable 3D printer and make a copy of the key. Glitzenhammer's building has exceptional security, but that won't keep Mako out of the townhouse—she can run the Baltimore Backdoor con in her sleep.

A thorough search through Marco's personal and corporate tax records last year revealed not only the existence of the love nest, but the purchase of a Rhino 815, a state-of-the-art safe guaranteed impregnable to everyone but the owner and the Rhino security team—and Mako, who coded a backdoor into Rhino's corporate computer system six months ago when she posed as a consultant.

We know that the Rhino is installed in Glitzenhammer's love nest, but what we don't know is what's *in* the safe. If this con is going to work, I'm counting on their being two specific items in that Rhino. One of them is a bikini.

The Glitzz Fantasy Bikini is a two-million-dollar swimsuit

horridly bedecked in precious gems and stones. Glitzenhammer designs and makes a new suit by hand in secret each year and unveils it to kick off the GlitzzShow, the company's annual presentation of next year's line.

Tomorrow is the start of the show. Given that Glitzenhammer keeps the swimsuit hidden away until the unveiling, I'm certain that it isn't at Glitzz headquarters—a place where secrets go to die—and I know that it's not in his sprawling West Roxbury mansion. The bikini has to be in the safe.

Yellowtail's voice crackles in my ear. "Octopus in 30."

"Scatter," I reply. Each team member responds with a single click. Coral, Yellowtail, and Marlin will meet up with Mako at the love nest. The four of them will split the bikini's jewels and anything else they want to lug out. My take will be the second item that I'm counting on being in the safe—the Glitzz corporate secrets that will allow me to control Marco Glitzenhammer and his Glitzz empire like a puppet for years to come.

I close my laptop and slide it into my bag. I stash my earpiece and microphone as well, then drain the Shiraz and gaze longingly at the empty crostini plate.

The maître d' walks Glitzenhammer over to my table. "This city is becoming unbearable," he grumbles as he sits. "A loud foreigner crashed her car outside. I couldn't even properly valet!"

"How awful, Marco," I reply.

The maître d' beckons to a waiter, who scurries over. "The usual," Glitzenhammer says before the man can speak.

Everyone on my team has their preferred cons. Now me, I love running the Avenging Annie con. It can take years, but in the end, the payoff is always worth it.

"Very good, sir," the waiter replies, then turns to me. "And for you, Mrs. Glitzenhammer?"

NAIL THE ENDING

I like to write "short short" stories, with word counts of under a thousand words to about 2,000 words. Those can be called "flash fiction," a loose term that can mean under a thousand words or under 1,500 words, depending on where you read the definition. There is a lot of subjectivity in writing definitions!

Even flash fiction stories still must have all the tenets of a successful story: a structure, a plot, a point of view, some kind of tension and conflict, a resolution, and so forth. This story is just over a thousand words long, with a light tone and focused on one character watching the caper she's masterminded unfold, so it wasn't enough to just have it her watch a successful caper—I wanted a last line that landed with a solid punch and added a twist to the story.

Some readers will see that punch coming, some will not. Here, our main character knows a lot about Marco and we don't know how, but as the caper unfolds, we know that she and team have done a lot of research, like an episode of the TV show *Leverage*, which focused on a team of con artists who take revenge on the greedy. It's only with the last line that we learn what the Avenging Annie long-con involves and how she was able to learn all of Marco's secrets.

When you are working on a short story that involves a plot twist, it's important to get that twist's timing right. Usually it's going to have to come in the last third of the story to be a twist, and the shorter the story, the harder that can be to get right, because you have a small number of words to build up the first two-thirds of the story to portray as the "normal" and "expected" for there even to be a twist that works at the end.

In those cases, finding a way to work that twist into the last line can delight your readers. If so, the pre-work has to be figuring out that twist when you create the story—you probably won't just stumble upon it when you're writing. Here, I knew I wanted to write about a funny little heist and give everyone seafood code names, then I figured out that the team's leader was going to be the key to the long con, then I thought up the twist and wrote toward that.

Most short stories aren't constructed to need a twisty, punchy last line, but for those that are, we want that punch to be solid and believable, producing a "wow!" in our readers instead of a "huh?" or a "meh." Here, I think I got it right. If our main character was just someone Marco worked with, that would be more of a "meh." If she was someone Marco had never met before, it would probably be a "huh?"

Also, ending a story with a great last line is really fun to write.

A great example of a punchy line (but not a last line) was when Luke Skywalker first heard the words, "No, I am your father." As viewers, we were like, how could this poor farming boy, a random kid, be the son of the galaxy's biggest villain? Luke doesn't believe it, but Darth Vader implores Luke to search his feelings. We start piecing together what we've learned over the first two films at the same Luke does, and we realize that huh, maybe it is true. If those drips of backstory weren't there, the line would have been met with ridicule by the audience, but they are there, so the line lands solidly. If the line had come in the first film, we wouldn't believe it.

However, that last line also has to walk the line between being unexpected by the reader *and* making sense from the story. It can't come out of nowhere. For instance, in this story, if I hadn't dropped clues that the main character knew details about Marco's love nest, or hadn't shown them having a relaxed conversation, that line would have landed with a thud. If that Darth Vader line had come in the first movie, where Darth and Luke hadn't interacted much and both Luke and Leia's characters weren't that complex, the line would have been met with laughter from the audience.

You might be revising a story when a great last line pops into your head—something twisty and perfect, something readers will love. Great! Go through the story and make sure it will actually make sense to the readers once they read it and can process it. It's like the big reveal in *The Sixth Sense*—most of us didn't see it coming during our first watch, but during our second watch, we looked for all the things we missed and were able to spot all the clues, and that made the reveal even more fun.

Readers remember well-written short stories for many reasons—beautiful words, great characters, fun plot. Often, they'll remember the ending if it's a story that demands a surprise or twisty ending, so if you can nail that ending with a fantastic last line, go for it!

Lesson learned: some stories are best ended with a solid, twisty last line—but it's got to be both unexpected and make perfect sense.

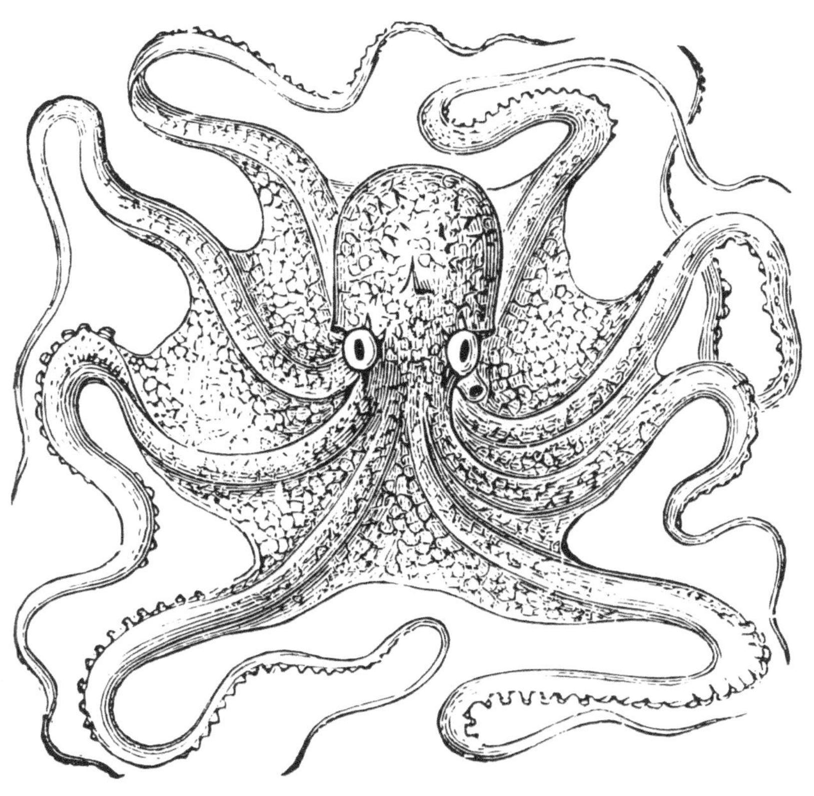

DRAGON'S LAIR

The garish Fabulosa Electronics sign blinks in the midday sun as Mom and I sit in my car in the store's parking lot.

"The owner is Ben Gonsalves," I say as we go over the plan again. "He'll be watching you on the security cameras. He'll come out of his office and stop you when he thinks he's figured it out."

"He's not going to figure it out," she replies. Then, in a rare moment of humility from Mom, she adds, "Thanks for setting this up for me, Gem."

"Anything for Stony Greyhill." Mom arches an eyebrow. She's heard that phrase often from those she'd later dupe. Stony Greyhill engenders loyalty, but she rarely pays it back.

"Fair warning," I continue, "there are cameras all over the place now. The world has changed while you were away."

"But people don't change," she replies. "They never do."

When my dad deserted me and my mom, we both dropped his last name. Dad's back in my life now, but I am my mother's daughter, a Greyhill through and through.

Mom was in prison for nine years, convicted of

masterminding a theft ring that spanned eleven states and several countries. A pyramid of purloining, the prosecutor had said smugly at Mom's trial. I thought the phrase was stupid then, but I'm a newspaper gal now. Words are my tools. Deception and guile are Mom's tools.

Okay, so maybe I'm not always my mother's daughter.

"I'm running The Dragon's Lair," she says. "It's the most impressive dodge for this."

"You mean it's the most showy dodge."

She fixes her granite-gray eyes on me. "Today is all about show."

I sigh. "Where do you want me?"

"Anywhere. Nowhere. I don't need help. I'm here to prove to this Gonsalves fellow that I can do this."

And she needs to prove it to me as well.

***

There are three things everyone should know about Stony Greyhill:

a. When she walks into a room, she draws every eye, soaks up all the attention—but only if she wants to. Other times, she's invisible—you'd never know she was there.
b. She's never ruined anyone's life unless they deserve it.
c. If you don't watch her hands, you'll miss everything.

***

I walk through the sliding doors into Fabulosa and settle in front of a display of cheap headphones, figuring that out of everything in the store, Mom will leave those alone.

She enters the store a few minutes later and gets to work. Sometimes her head is up, shoulders back, radiating confidence. Sometimes she slumps and shuffles, submissive, becoming part of the background. But her eyes are always moving, and her hands are always moving.

After ten minutes, she approaches a sales associate, the one closest to me. "Tell Mr. Gonsalves that Stony Greyhill is done," she says dismissively. The associate gave her a quizzical look. "Just go," Mom adds with a shooing motion. The associate shrugs, then walks to a rear door marked Employees Only.

Mom strides over to me. "How much did you see?" she asks as she ties her long blonde hair into a ponytail.

"Enough. Nice lair."

The associate returns, then leads us back through the employee door and into Ben Gonsalves's office, where we remain standing.

"I'm confused, Ms. Greyhill," Gonsalves says to Mom. "I thought this would take a lot longer."

"First," Mom says, ignoring the remark, "I'm going to show you what I'm carrying. And what I'm not carrying." She empties her pockets, placing everything on Gonsalves's desk: a pair of tweezers, the ends filed sharp; three elastic bands; four paperclips; two eight-inch squares of aluminum foil, folded into triangles; and a set of nail clippers, one large, one small.

"But where's all the stuff?" Gonsalves asks.

***

Two months ago, a month before her sentence was up, I visited Mom and brought in a copy of my latest newspaper article, a fluffy profile on Ben Gonsalves and Fabulosa Electronics.

"He's a nice guy. And he told me, off the record, that his store is getting hammered on costs," I said.

"Why?"

"Trying to stave off the bigger chains and the online stores. But mostly it's shortage. Theft, bad inventory processes, dumb warehouse people. But mostly theft."

"Huh," Mom said. Then she got that look, the one that means her gears were already turning.

I'd been on her to go straight once she got out. Not begging, because begging never works on a Greyhill. The Fabulosa idea had been all hers. I just planted the idea, then helped set this up.

***

"I'm confused," Gonsalves repeats. "I watched you the whole time. But you've got nothing on you."

Mom turns to me, the hint of a smile crossing her lips. "Show him the lair."

Sighing, I lead us back to the sales floor and over to a far corner of the store. "Look in that refrigerator," I say, pointing to a display. Gonsalves opens the door, revealing a stack of display laptops and tablets, along with a pile of broken anti-theft devices and a few security cameras.

Gonsalves shakes his head. "I barely saw you in this part of the store. How did you carry all this—"

Mom cuts him off, gesturing at the pile. "You can't rely solely on technology. Preventing shortage is all about people and processes. I'll teach your staff how to read people. I'll look at your systems, sure. I'll improve how you warehouse your stock. But *real* security—that's all people."

"I can't pay a lot," Gonsalves says.

Mom turns to me as she answers him. "The money's not important. I want to do the right thing for once."

We Greyhills aren't maudlin folk, so before I tear up, I tell Mom that I'll wait in the car while she and Gonsalves talk things through.

Ben Gonsalves might have found his savior, I think as I head for the door. But if I could give him some advice, it would be this: when you find yourself saying "Anything for Stony Greyhill"—watch her hands, and watch your pockets.

BUILD RELATIONSHIPS QUICKLY

In short short stories, there's not a lot of room for extensive world building. When a story focuses on relationships, like this one does, it's important to drop in just enough information that the reader can picture the relationship without you explaining the history of the relationship.

In just about a thousand words, we learn that Stony is a con woman who's gone to jail and has been released, and that Gem rejected the life to go straight but hasn't fully turned her back on the con. Her dad deserted Gem and her mom, he's back in their life, and Gem has been trying to find a way to help Stony get acclimated to life after prison.

That's about all the room I had for backstory. It felt odd to drop all that in in one place, so I decided to drop the pieces here and there, enough so that by the time Stony was working the Dragon's Lair con, we knew about all we needed to know about their mother-daughter relationship, and we could then sit back and see how Gem reacted to Stony moving about the store.

I had a choice to make early when I thought of this story: would the point of view character be Stony or Gem? (The point of view character is the character through whose eyes the story is being told—I talk a lot more about point of view later in this book). If it was Stony, I'd be focusing on her minute-by-minute movements in the store, which might be interesting, but I didn't like telling the backstory of their relationship from her point of view. I liked telling it better from Gem's point of view.

The lesson I learned from this story is that when I'm writing about relationships, I don't need to paint that part of the story with a lot of paint and a thick brush. I can use a fine brush and just a little paint here and there, then step back as I write and decide if I've done enough. If I haven't, I can add a detail or two. If I feel like I've painted too heavily, like I'm bogging the reader down with information they don't need, I'll go back and delete anything unneeded. Especially with short stories, I try to lean on being an efficient writer, one who trusts my readers to make connections if I give them enough information and the right information.

I tried to do this in the earlier stories. Paul and Jason have an easy back and forth relationship in "Ride Captain Ride," and Jason can then quickly pick up on the fact that something is off with Paul—I don't need to have Jason explicitly state that he and Paul normally can talk about anything, have been "friends" for a long time, and the like. In "500 Words," I was limited by the word count, and since the story was about an affair, and these two people knew each other very well, I could not have them waste any words—their relationship had to become clear solely through their dialogue.

In "Avenging Annie," the main character is short and efficient in her speech with her team members—she can picture what each will do, but simply tells each to "go" when it's time, and this hopefully gives the impression that she trusts each of them, that they've been doing this for a while, and that has little to worry about.

Whenever you have more than one character in a scene, you have a relationship, whether the people have known each other for decades or seconds. When you buy a coffee, you may observe the person making your coffee and ringing up your transaction, and you'll notice if something is off—you are building a very short-term relationship built on the trust that they won't poison you or steal your money. They might be doing the same—will they turn around and find that you ordered a coffee and left, and they've worked for nothing except a coffee that they now have to throw out?

Here, Stony and Gem have a pre-existing relationship. Stony is sizing up Gonsalves, Gonsalves is sizing up Stony, and Gem and Gonsalves already have a relationship, but it doesn't really come into play here.

We are humans, and we are wired (usually) to trust initially —it's our default setting, and it's hard to override that and replace distrust as our default. I see that attempted a lot in my clients' fiction—the character who trusts no one—but the idea of a character trusting no one often comes across as false unless the writer has done an amazing job of character building.

In your writing, you'll have a main character or two that you'll build your story around. That character will have relationships with all the other characters; those relationships will change over the course of the story. They'll also make new relationships with new characters. Think about how you want those pre-existing relationships to feel when the story starts, and how you want and need them to change as the story progresses. Then think about how new characters will react to these pre-existing relationships and how they might change them or have to adapt to them.

The shorter the story, the less time you'll have for things to change, most likely, and the less time you'll have to inform the reader about the relationships. Like I had to do here with Stony and Gem, you may have to drop the reader directly into a relationship, so make sure you know that relationship well enough to describe it to readers and still make it feel authentic.

Lesson learned: drop the reader into pre-existing character relationships quickly, and make those relationships feel natural.

FLY IN DANISH

Flit perched on a dusty jade plant, frustrated. There was nothing wonderful to eat in this house. After all the effort that it had taken to get *in* the house yesterday, Flit had hoped for something at least slightly memorable. The best she had done was nibble on a stray nugget of Nasty-dog's kibble.

Kibble was *not* memorable.

But then the human opened the refrigerator, took out a paper bag—and Flit's world exploded.

She sensed sugar. Apple. Cinnamon. Dough.

And all of those things were wonderful.

The human placed the Danish on a plate and turned toward the coffee maker on the counter.

The intoxicating scent, coupled with typical housefly hunger, made Flit uncharacteristically careless, and she flew straight at the treasure, ignoring the human, her compound eyes locked on her prize, the pastry growing closer, more intoxicating—

Movement from the rear!

Flit dived up and to her right as the human's gigantic hand

came down and past her, slapping the table instead of her fragile body.

She took a quick buzz around the kitchen, then flew into the adjoining dining room and hung upside down from the ceiling, grooming herself as she planned her next move.

Perhaps the human would drop crumbs on the floor. A single crumb of pastry outweighed a bowlful of Nasty-dog's horrific food.

But crumbs were no treasure. A pastry—now that was a prize.

Flit crawled across the ceiling, hung from the door frame, and peered into the kitchen.

The upside-down human was eating the Danish—and far too neatly! There were no crumbs! And half of the pastry was already gone!

Movement from behind!

Flit jump-pivoted to reverse direction. Nasty-dog looked up at her. It wagged its tail.

It was mocking her!

She dismissed Nasty-dog's effrontery and pivoted back to face the kitchen. Houseflies survive by scavenging or theft— and stolen food is far sweeter than found food.

The human left the remaining Danish resting on the plate while it drank its coffee. The scent of the pastry washed over Flit. She analyzed the odors. Prioritized them.

Soft pastry—easier to eat when moist, so time was of the essence. Glazed sugar—perfect for quick bursts of energy. Chunks of apple smothered in a cinnamon-laced gel— ideal for—

Yes. The gel. That was the *real* prize. Flit's feeding tube twitched in anticipation.

But would the human leave any gel? Sugar slabs and pastry crumbs were worthy fare, but Flit was not a housefly who settled. She had been the biggest maggot in her clutch—and had successfully laid six clutches of healthy eggs herself—because she *did not settle.* In the world of houseflies, size went hand-in-hand-in-hand-in-hand-in-hand-in-hand with how well one fed. And to feed well, one never settled.

Flit craved that Danish—especially that gooey filling, rife with pectin and sucrose and preservatives—as much as she'd craved anything in her 22 days of life.

It would be hers.

The human grabbed the Danish, took another bite, and plopped the remaining morsel onto the plate as it again reached for its coffee.

The human was eating too quickly!

Decision time.

Flit could wait for the human to finish. Perhaps it would leave a few particles, and she could feed decently, if not glamorously—

No. Scouring was for settlers. Flit quivered in anger.

She would not end her crusade. She would not settle.

The human stood up, coffee cup in hand. It turned and walked to the sink. Away from the table. Away from the plate.

Away from the Danish.

Decision made.

Flit slid a foreleg over her antennae, ensuring that they were grit-free and optimized for flight guidance. Then she jumped, performed a barrel roll to right herself, whisked to the table, and landed ten inches from her prize.

The human's back was still to her. It was adding something to its coffee—a different sugar, Flit sensed, one inferior to the pastry's sugar glaze, but its scent momentarily tempted her. Perhaps she could wait for the human to leave, scoop up a few spilt granules—

No. She would not be led astray by specks of inferior sweetness. Not when a Danish was in play.

She jump-hopped three inches closer. The human was still at the counter.

Flit shivered with joy. Success was close at wing!

She stepped closer still to the plate. The aroma was all-consuming. The hairs on her legs bristled in anticipation.

She was about to claim her prize.

Flit planned the next few seconds. She'd land on the center of whatever the human had left and stomp on any remaining apple filling with her feet. Since she tasted with her toes, she'd spend a few microseconds basking in the glow of success and sweetness.

Then she'd lower her feeding tube into the cinnamon gel. The filling was most likely viscous enough so that she could draw it into her feeding tube without delay, but if the slurry was too thick, she'd simply vomit a drop of stomach acid out of her tube onto the goo and break the mixture down enough so that she could slurp it back up.

A solid plan for a delicious and well-earned treasure.

Movement from above! Movement from the left!

The human. Its back was no longer turned. It was next to the table.

Its huge hand was coming down at her!

Humans foolishly swat directly at flies, so Flit did what all flies do—she jumped forward, then veered, the air from the failed swat gently propelling her, the *thwack* of the human's meaty hand on the table startling Nasty-dog into an insipid barking frenzy.

Flit landed on the ceiling and schemed as the human shook its fist at her.

So close to the prize, yet thwarted once again!

The human stared up at her, its hands on its hips, its huge

face peering up at her, filling her thousands of simple eyes with its single simple expression.

Flit scrubbed her two front legs together, then preened, waiting for the human's next move. It was standing between Flit and the Danish. Flit could easily dodge the human and zip over to the plate, but she'd have no time to feed before the next predictable and ineffective attack.

It was a standoff. And Flit never backed down from a standoff.

Predictably, the human broke first. It turned, picked up the Danish, and—

No!

It was reaching for the door!

It was leaving!

With the remains of *her* Danish!

Flit quickly analyzed the situation. Human at door, hand almost on doorknob. Nasty-dog sitting on the floor near the door, tail wagging, facing the human. Human holding Danish.

There was precious little time. She had to make a move. She had one chance.

Of course. The Parabola Pounce! But could she pull it off?

Houseflies are a boasting lot. Flit normally discounted their tales of inflated prowess. Besides, showboating flies were always scrawny in comparison to her—if they could *really* achieve such feats of derring-do, would they not have looked more fit? More lustrous? Braggart flies were killed or caught once their egos got as big as their stories.

But she had heard all the tales of flies who'd *supposedly* performed the Parabola Pounce—a maneuver of legend, a legend passed down over thousands of housefly generations by solemn elders.

Flit wasn't convinced that the Parabola Pounce had *ever* been successfully performed. But if ever there was a time to try a legendary and possibly impossible maneuver, it was now. For a Danish.

Flit made her move.

She rocketed at Nasty-dog and landed on its nose, facing its eyes.

Nasty-dog's eyes grew wide, then its head tilted skyward. Flit had assumed—correctly, of course—that the beast would try to eat her. She then took off as the beast sprang. Nasty-dog bashed into the human, who was by now halfway out the door, back turned.

Flit deftly avoided the mash of dog-jaws and continued to the doorway, finishing her parabola and landing upside-down on the casing.

The human, not expecting Nasty-dog to lunge from behind, stumbled.

It dropped the pastry on the stairs.

The outside stairs!

Yes! Flit's circulatory tube throbbed in glee, and she flew outside through the doorway to a hedge to compose herself. The Parabola Pounce was not simply the stuff of legends after all! She had manipulated both the dog and the human into doing exactly what she wanted! Oh, swarms would gather to hear her recount this day. She would regale the throngs, ending with the moment she first stepped into that cinnamon slop, sucking the—

The human picked up the remnants of the Danish, walked into the house, and closed the door behind it.

No!

Her treasure was gone!

She flew to the steps. No crumbs. Not even the tiniest smear of gel.

She flew angrily to the door and buzz-bopped into the side

windows, two times, five times, a dozen times, unleashing her wrath upon the human's house.

This could not happen! What was the human going to do with a dropped Danish? It wouldn't eat it. Most humans did not ingest food that they had dropped on the ground. Most humans never even *foraged* for food. What would this human do with the pastry? Discard it? Or, even worse, give it to Nasty-dog?

The horror. She mourned her Danish's demise.

Wait—the human. *It* was responsible for her loss. Each of her eight thousand simple eyes narrowed as her mourning turned to fury.

She would make the human pay. But how?

She was still pondering several arcane methods when the human emerged from the house two minutes later. It closed and locked the door behind it (goodbye, Nasty-dog!) and strode toward—the garage.

Garages were places of wicked delights and unholy terrors.

Garages were places of spiders.

The garage door was open, so Flit flew slowly inside the dark space, tracking the human while deftly avoiding the sides of the structure.

She braced herself against the siren song of the spiders. She had seen too many friends perish in the clutches of those monsters. Spiders were everywhere flies needed to be, and their powers of persuasion were insidious. The evil webbed ones drew flies in with hypnotic chants that only their prey could hear, and the insidious mobile spiders—the stalkers, the walkers, the ones who did not need webs to secure their prey— those fiends jeered and catcalled, weakening a fly's resolve until it dropped to the ground—to be consumed.

Flit continued to fly as the webbed ones chanted their songs of death. The horrible eight-legged striders shrieked and whooped. Flit shut out their siren songs and landed on a bag of mulch.

The human opened the car door.

There was no time to fully develop a plan. Revenge, in whatever form it took, would have to occur *inside* the car.

But Flit had never been inside a car. It was unthinkable for a housefly to willingly enter a car. The rational part of her tiny brain screamed at her: *Let the human leave! Do not enter a car! Find pickings elsewhere!*

Ordinarily, Flit listened intently to the rational part of her brain, and that had served her well—after all, she was still alive, in a world bent on housefly destruction. But she pictured the dropped Danish, wallowed in the memory of its scent, and again felt rage at being denied her prize.

She flew directly at the car door.

Which the human pulled shut a second before she got there.

Flit deftly banked to the left and slipped over the car's hood, her rudimentary nervous system racing.

Denied again! Damn this wily human!

Flit perched on an inside windowsill, demoralized, not even bothering to check for spiders, as the car started up and began reversing out of the garage.

What to do? The human was leaving, and a quick glance at the garbage bin showed that its lid was secured, trapping any potential runner-up treats inside.

All her planning. All her questing.

All her failing.

The garage grew dimmer. The door was closing!

Flit had spent too much time stewing in her own juices. She needed to leave. Now. Or she would be trapped in the garage with the soul-sucking spiders. She was growing weak from hunger and exertion, and she would eventually succumb if she spent too much time here.

Spiders preyed on weakness. Weakness is how flies died.

With supreme effort, Flit launched herself off the mulch bag and headed for the closing door, diving under the rubber gasket and its tendrils of dead webs and dried leaves just before it shut.

Back in the bright outside world, Flit flew up and circled the driveway.

The human's car slowed its reverse, stopped, and began to drive forward.

The human was escaping!

Flit made a beeline for the car. The vehicle inched down the driveway and paused at the bottom, waiting for an opening in traffic.

Flit buzzed around the car's rear. She could sense no opening. The top of the car also yielded no entry.

There! The human had left a side window down on the passenger side. Just a crack, but the gap looked large enough for her to squeeze into.

She worked up to speed, correctly judged her vector, and zoomed at the gap.

Microseconds before she entered, the car pulled onto the street. Flit, buffeted by the sudden push of air, slammed onto the street.

She lay stunned on the pavement, feet pointed to the sky, the world turning from black to gray and then mercifully to her normal mosaic of thousands of flickering images. She righted herself, then shook to clear her head.

The car was gone!

As was the wily Danish-stealing human!

She probed the air. Nothing. No residual sweetness, no wafts of cinnamon, no hint of pastry.

No treasure.

Waves of depression washed over, followed by waves of resignation.

And then waves of anger.

How dare the human run away! But should she give up, or give chase?

She considered the options. If she gave up, she could spend a lazy day scouring the human's yard for treats. Admittedly, there was always something for a fly to consume—humans were messy, and all other creatures defecated or died outside. Most flies were not picky. Flit could chalk this venture up to a near-success, revel in the glory of the successful Parabola Pounce, and go on about her fly-business—if she was willing to scavenge. To settle.

But that Danish. Such a loss.

No. Flit would *not* give up. She would give *chase*.

Fifteen seconds after being pushed to the ground by the roiling air currents, she flew. Ten feet up, she banked to the right and followed the road.

She would track down that crafty human.

The world of a fly is a small one. Flit could not see clearly for more than a few yards. Everything beyond that distance was a wall of dark and light blotches. But she knew which way the car had traveled.

She dipped lower, five feet above the road, three feet, two feet—

Movement from behind!

She veered to the right as a car whizzed by. She was caught in its wake and pin wheeled, but to her surprise, she tumbled *forward*. She struggled to maintain a straight path as she pondered what had just happened.

How could she have moved forward so much faster than in ordinary flight?

The car...the air...the direction...Her miniscule brain worked as hard as any fly's brain ever had, and the realization of what she had just done astonished her.

This was how she could gain ground on the human. She would use the air currents from the cars to gain on the thief-human's car!

Flit's simple heart swelled with pride. Surely, she was the first of her kind to use cars in such a fashion! Between this maneuver and the Parabola Pounce, she was breaking new ground as a housefly. She would be remembered along with all the greats.

Then her failure with the Danish hit her. No, her story was not yet ready to be told. Only after she had achieved her ultimate revenge could she delight the masses with her exploits.

She continued her car-assisted travel, flying straight, getting passed by a car, surfing the air to shoot ahead of it.

Was she making up distance? Or had each car that passed been the same car? Would she even recognize the correct car? Most likely, no other car contained a human who had recently eaten a Danish. She would find her victim through scent and smarts.

The car next to her slowed, then stopped.

She flew up and over the cars, trying to recall every detail about the Danish-car.

Not this one. Too dark.

Not the next. Too short.

Not the next. It had no roof. But was she positive that the human's car had had no roof? She had been stunned on the pavement, and houseflies have no need for perfect recall.

She buzzed down, mere inches above the human inside the car, and combed the air for scents.

A coffee smell—but different than the Danish-human's coffee. A waft of tobacco. No, this was not the right car.

She alighted on the hood of the roofless car and stared at the car ahead of her.

The color looked about right. The size looked about right.

Could it be?

She took off and flew around to the side.

A gap. On the passenger side window.

Success! She flew in a quick series of circles, celebrating.

She had found the Danish-car! Oh, the majesty of a successful hunt! Soon she would wreak havoc on—

The car accelerated.

Flit dived for the gap, but the wind from the car's sudden movement drove her back.

She strained against the gust, flying as hard as she could before the car gained too much distance, and landed with a tiny thump on the back of the crafty-human's car, nestling on the gasket where the trunk met the window.

She scrabbled for purchase, hooked her front legs onto the rubber seam, and tucked her body down to avoid the slipstream of air rushing above her.

She would wait until the car came to a stop again, then she would enter and collect her spoils.

But first, she needed to rest. The flight had exhausted her.

Movement to her left!

A dragonfly! Less than a foot away!

It gripped the rear window. Its twin eye-orbs glittered as it slowly raised and lowered its wings.

Flit froze in fear.

Dragonflies were the alpha predators of the insect world. Too wily to be trapped in a spider's web, too agile to fear attack from other flying killers, dragonflies chilled the quasi-blood of all insects—including houseflies.

There are many ways for a fly to die. Birds ate them. Glue traps and abandoned webs starved them. Humans squashed them and sprayed them. Nearly every other member of the animal kingdom feasted joyously on their newborn maggots.

But dragonflies—they were a terror beyond all other terrors.

They approached swiftly and silently, appearing from nowhere as if spirits. It was the rare fly who lived to recount an escape from a dragonfly's clutches.

There was something else about dragonflies that Flit had heard, something she couldn't recall…

The dragonfly tapped its abdomen-tail on the window to get Flit's attention.

"Why are you on this vehicle, fly?" the dragonfly whispered. "You have made a terrible mistake, my future meal."

Flit shivered but steeled herself against the words. What *was* it that the elder had said about dragonflies? It had been ten days since she and a dozen other females had gathered to lay eggs on a dead squirrel while an elder imparted wisdom. It was hard for Flit to remember events from ten minutes ago, let alone ten days ago. That was half a lifetime, and that elder had surely turned to dust by now. What was it…

"Look, fly, at my wings slowly raising and lowering," the dragonfly droned. "Be entranced by them. Be struck motionless in fear. When this vehicle stops, I will pounce on you, and you shall be mine, just like so many of your kind before you."

Words. The elder had said *something* about dragonfly words.

"It is fortuitous that you landed here," the beast continued, chuckling. "I have yet to feed today. Before this vehicle stops I will feed upon *you*, and slake my thirst and hunger by drinking your quasi-blood."

Then Flit recalled the elder's proclamation: *The silent dragonfly is light and deadly. The talking dragonfly is weighed down by its pomposity.*

Flit adjusted her grip, hooking all three right legs onto the rubber seam so she could swivel toward the dragonfly—and used her left three legs to make a universally-rude gesture.

The predator gasped, pounding its abdomen-tail against the glass. "Such insolence in one so doomed!" the dragonfly hissed.

"Your final hour approaches, maiden fly, and whatever clutch you last laid shall surely be your last!"

Although the dragonfly was unable to attack while the car was moving, once it stopped, Flit would be no match for the killer. Her only hope was that the dragonfly would be too full of talk to make its move before Flit could escape into the car.

The car slowed.

Flit prepared to jump. The dragonfly bent its legs, preparing to do the same.

Flit's timing would have to be impeccable, or she would die on this car.

The car stopped.

Flit and the dragonfly both prepared to pounce—

Movement from above!

Something huge!

Flit pressed her body onto the metal of the car's trunk to shrink herself from this new horror.

A sparrow cupped its wings to halt its progress as it landed next to her, its huge talons gripping the lip of the trunk. A tremendous wing smashed against the car's window, the primary flight feathers missing Flit by half an inch.

Flit, still paralyzed by terror, prepared for the end. She could not shut her eyes, so she looked away instead, saddened that her quest for the Danish had failed. To be consumed by a bird was an unceremonious end. She wondered if she'd feel any—

She heard a scream.

The sparrow swung its massive head around to face Flit, the dragonfly wedged between the bird's upper and lower mandibles.

The bird cocked its head as it gazed at Flit. It trilled something, then launched off the car and into the sky with its meal.

Flit was no expert in bird-speak, but she could have sworn the sparrow had warbled, "Dragonflies talk way too much."

The only good bird was a dead bird. Every fly knew that mantra from the moment it could wriggle. Birds could never be defeated, only avoided.

But this bird had saved Flit's life. One day, she vowed, she would return the favor to another bird.

Back to matters at hands.

By now, Flit was weak from overexertion and lack of food. She needed shelter. She needed to get inside the car. The Danish was gone. Her quest was no longer about claiming her ultimate prize. And perhaps it was no longer about revenge.

Her quest was now about survival.

Flit grasped the rubber seam with her left foreleg and twisted around so she could jump into flight and make it to the window.

But she didn't have the energy. She needed to rest. She needed to recover from this latest near-death experience. Once she—

The car began moving.

Flit silently screamed in frustration. Foiled again by this human and this car!

She rued the time she had spent dwelling on the sparrow sparing her. Surely the bird would have eaten her if it weren't for the dragonfly. Birds could not be trusted! Flit now promised to lay wrath upon all feathered beings.

If she survived.

The car accelerated. The air rushed over the top of the vehicle and down the back window, battering Flit as she desperately clutched the gasket.

The sun beat on her. The wind slapped at her. The metal trunk burned her. Flit found a small gap between the seam and the trunk, and dragged her body into it. Beyond the gap lay darkness.

Where would it lead? What lay beyond the dark? Spiders, most likely. They loved the darkness, the cowards.

But she had to risk it. She couldn't stay exposed any longer. She needed to rest.

Flit started to hallucinate. Her previous three meals—unfortunately, all scavenged meals—floated in front of her.

The orange rind, covered with ants and mulch. She drove away the vile scavengers by buzzing her wings until they grew frustrated, then feasted on the sweet citrus.

The ice cream, dropped on the sidewalk by a tiny-human. She sucked on the congealing vanilla mass before the sun dried it up.

The red cup, tumbling in yesterday's wind. She chased it until it came to rest against a poplar. The inside was coated with cola droplets.

Wait. Cups. Coffee cups. Crafty-human drank coffee from a cup. While eating *her* Danish—the Danish that had been *stolen* from her.

Flit's hallucinations evaporated. She would not give up.

She would not settle.

She settled against the lip of the trunk. The car shook and shuddered as it sped along the road.

Then the words of an elder came back to her: *Woe to the fly whose reach exceeds its grasp.*

Flit dipped her antennae in sorrow. The elder had been correct. Flit had successfully completed the Parabola Pounce, and had used the wake of cars to travel faster than flight, but those feats were slim consolation. She had escaped death half a dozen times today, but for what?

Pride. Pride was her downfall. And pride would be the end of her, here, wedged in a gap on a car going who knows where.

She was exhausted, and nearly starved, and beaten down with loss—loss of the Danish, and soon, loss of her life, for if she did not eat or drink soon, she would surely die.

She dwelled on the morose for twenty minutes, too lost in her black thoughts to notice when the car stopped, too glum to notice when the human opened the car door and left, too melancholy to notice—

That smell. What was that smell?

The air was barely moving, but Flit, highly attuned to delectable scents, detected something overpowering.

Rich. Sweet. Luscious.

She shook to clear her head, then sampled the air again.

It was akin to the long-gone Danish, only multiplied a thousand-fold.

Flit crawled out from the gap and onto the trunk, ignoring the heat, momentarily blinded by the harsh sunlight.

The world was *filled* with Danish-scent.

But how? And where was it coming from? And how could so much goodness exist in such a harsh world?

She tentatively attempted flight, but dropped to the parking lot. She no longer had the energy to take wing.

So she hopped.

She headed into the slight breeze, and hopped along the pavement, an inch at a time, toward the source of the smell.

The scent grew stronger. Flit plodded along the hot asphalt, drawing on strength she never knew she had. Ten minutes after starting her arduous journey from the car, she collapsed against a shadowed wall, exhausted, her energy all but spent.

Movement from the front!

She tensed, prepared to deal with yet another danger. What would be next? A human? A bird? Yes, it would probably be a bird. How fitting to be saved by a bird, only to be eaten by a bird.

But it was not a bird or a human.

It was a housefly.

He hopped over to Flit. "Who are you, weary stranger?" the housefly asked, cautiously holding up its two forelegs to show that it meant no harm.

"I am Flit. I have had a terrible day, full of danger and loss, and I am seeking respite." She struggled to her feet and spread her two forelegs wide in a welcoming return gesture. "I am overwhelmed by heavenly smells. Where am I? What *is* this place?"

The other housefly took flight and performed celebratory loops in front of a propped-open screen door. Above the door was an old wooden sign, white with red lettering. Neither fly saw the colors, and they couldn't make any sense of the words painted on the sign: "Delivery Entrance for Stueflue's Bakery."

The housefly landed next to Flit. His antennae trembled in glee.

"This is nirvana."

KEEP YOUR CHARACTERS IN PERIL!

I had signed up for a class about writing pulp fiction (not the movie, but the genre), where the main character is in constant, thrilling danger and the action is over the top. I can't remember why I decided that my main character should be a housefly, but it worked well enough, and this piece ended up selling and was printed in an anthology.

I went with a third-person point of view (we don't hear from Flit as "I" but "Flit"). The narrator does a lot of work in this story, describing Flit's actions and giving us a lot of Flit's thoughts (and using a lot of exclamation points—they are an emotional and subjective narrator!).

With pulpy fiction, bad things happen to the characters, they barely find ways out of danger, then more bad things happen, and the cycle keeps repeating as much as you like. I cut some scenes from the final version of this because the story was getting long—including Flit barely surviving a trip through the car wash!

Some genres require lots of over-the-top danger, like this one. One thing that authors can have a lot of trouble with: we can be too easy on our characters. We love our characters, and we know we have to create tension for readers to keep turning pages, but we hold back like protective parents even when we know it's not the right thing to do. We can't help ourselves!

Your character doesn't have to be shot at constantly. The peril can come from the weather, swarms of mosquitoes, the cold of outer space—really, anything that keeps them in constant danger and tension if you're writing in genres like pulp fiction and action adventure. You will need to give them the occasional break (this gives the reader the occasional break, too) because they will need to get OUT of that danger, but then it's on to more danger.

The danger and tension can also be internal—psychological, emotional, stressful, the "will they or won't they" of relationships. The key is that our main characters, no matter the genre or the plot, have to go through trials from the beginning of the story to the end, even in short stories. Here, Flit goes through a lot. In the earlier story "500 Words," one character thinks their long-term affair is over (again), when in fact the two characters have the chance to finally be together. In "Dragon's Lair," Stony's trials aren't severe in the story, but she has to use her old skills to prove that she's useful outside of the grifting life, so there's some pressure to succeed, as well as pressure to please her daughter.

For Flit, the pressures are mostly external. The dog, the car, the wind. There's also exhaustion, annoyance, and the fear of the spiders. Flit was a great character to put into a pulp story, because Flit has a very dramatic personality—her highs are very high and very immediate, and her lows are low and very immediate. She's not stoic, even when she thinks she is. She reacts in the moment.

So when we think about our characters and peril, first, we have to know what story we are writing and what genre our story fits in. For example, if you are writing a sweet romance, your characters shouldn't be fighting off constant gunfire— that's not what your audience is looking for. Instead, they will be fighting off misunderstanding, miscommunication, bad timing, and bad circumstances, along with a random event or two, like a trip and fall that forces them to miss the dinner with their future soulmate. That's their peril.

A thriller will have more external and more constant peril, more akin to what Flit faced in the pulp story—fail, barely succeed, face something even worse, succeed, face something even worse, and on and on until the end.

A drama will have peril and tension that often comes from relationships and both internal and external circumstances, some short-term, some long-term. A slapstick comedy can have "peril" come from all directions all the time, with that peril being over the top and ridiculous and usually external.

Whatever the genre, whatever the length of your story, your characters have to face some kind of peril, even if it's the most minor. In "Ride Captain Ride," Jason's peril is that Paul is hiding his emotions and it's annoying and ruining the afternoon, so he's got to figure out what is going on to succeed. In "Avenging

Annie," the con is going really well, but the peril could be that something doesn't work out, and because the main character's long con hinges on everything going right and Marco showing up at the restaurant exactly on time, there's some tension.

(Flit, however, faces the most true peril out of any character in this book, mostly because she doesn't live for very long and this story takes up a good percentage of her life!)

Bonus fun fact: the title of this story comes from the name of the bakery, Stueflue, which means "housefly" in Danish!

Lesson learned: keep your characters in peril—external or internal, major or minor—and don't go easy on them.

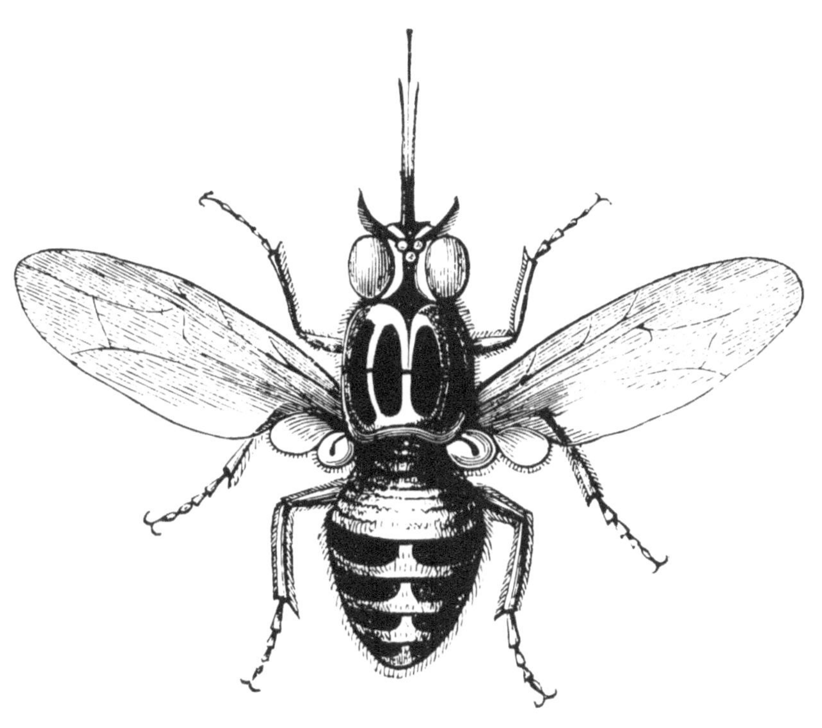

HOMAGE TO WILLIAM WYMARK JACOBS

"I found this box of your old stuff, Dad," my daughter Annie says. "Kayla, show Grandpa what's in the box."

Six-year-old Kayla dumps the box's contents on the rug near my bed and starts sifting through the contents.

A terminal illness has robbed me of both movement and speech, so I can't warn Annie and Kayla.

To my horror, Kayla grabs the green plastic toy soldier.

My eyes try and fail to go wide, and my heart pounds.

I could never bring myself to get rid of it. That toy soldier is my only link to Belinda, my first and greatest love.

My lost love.

***

Forty years ago, Belinda and I were biologists documenting the marine life around Kuzon-4, a massive, decommissioned oil rig halfway between South America and Antarctica. Three days before the structure was slated for demolition, the rest of our science team disembarked to a docked supply ship, leaving

Belinda and me with a few computers, a broken external communications console, and one submersible, a yellow bug-like underwater vehicle. We would stay to complete our observations and then depart via a Kuzon Corp. helicopter in three days.

Morris, the supply ship's captain, spoke to the two of us privately as his crew oversaw the debarkation. "Louis, Belinda, I want to thank you for your kindness by giving you this gift, although I'm not sure if I bring good or harm." From his coat pocket he withdrew a tiny plastic toy soldier, green, molded to catch the army man in the act of lobbing a grenade.

Morris pinched the toy between two fingers as if it were aflame. "This was given to me by my first captain many years ago," he continued in a solemn tone. "It grants the bearer three wishes and no more."

Belinda reached for the toy but stopped short of touching it. "Were your wishes granted?" she asked.

Morris nodded but looked sad. "Now I carry the soldier as a reminder of my fate. But perhaps you two will benefit from the toy's power. There are consequences to wishing, Belinda and Louis. May you wish better than I did." He handed the toy to me and left before we could ask him more.

That night, Belinda and I leaned against a support rail high atop the rig, the calm ocean below bathed in moonlight, a light breeze blowing Belinda's raven hair to and fro. She looked achingly beautiful. We laughed as we dismissed Morris's story as folly, although I did keep the soldier in my pocket as a souvenir.

Belinda's shoulder brushed mine, and my body thrummed, as it had with every innocuous touch from her over the last two years.

She sighed. "Oh, Louis. If only I had seen one." She was referring to a colossal squid. It was her lifelong quest to see one up close, but in dozens of dives in the submersible, she never had.

"We have three more days," I replied. "There's still time."

She sighed. "Do you know what it's like to be so close to what you want for so long but never getting it?"

I nodded. I had never worked up the courage to tell her what had been in my heart since we met two years ago; if I had, then everything would have turned out differently. Instead, I slipped my hand into my pocket and clutched the soldier. Although I didn't take Morris's story seriously, I wished anyway. *Let her see a colossal squid up close*, I thought. *That is my wish.*

The next day dawned bright and clear. Belinda climbed into the submersible, while I sat in the control room two hundred feet above her.

We went through our pre-mission checklist, ending it as we always did, with Belinda singing "*Meet me in St. Louis, Louis,*" a refrain from an old song that she loved, and me responding in kind, "*Meet me at the fair.*"

The submersible dived, circling the rig's immense underwater structure. All was normal until Belinda said, "Louis! Check the camera! Do you see it?"

I gripped the monitor. There it was: a colossal squid, its giant body framed in the submersible's headlights. The creature was huge, at least sixty feet long, its tentacles as thick as a man's body.

Belinda laughed and whooped as she angled the submersible for a better view, while I smiled, thrilled that I had helped make her dream come true.

Then the squid turned and slammed into the submersible, its tentacles beating against the hull. Belinda screamed while I watched the monitor in horror. The beast battered the sub until the glass observation bubble shattered, the video and audio feed cutting out in the middle of Belinda's cry for help.

I hurried down to the lowest observation deck and scanned the sea but saw nothing save for a yellow plastic panel bobbing in the waves. Dazed, I made my way back to the control room and tried to raise help on the radio, but the unit was still inoperable.

I wrapped my arms around my body and sobbed, then yanked the toy soldier from my pocket. I prepared to toss the toy in anger, then froze, mirroring the soldier's form. *Maybe she's not dead*, I thought. *Maybe I can still save her.*

I held the toy in my hand. *Let Belinda find her way back to me,* I thought. *That is my wish.*

Nothing.

I dropped the toy, then wallowed in grief—

—until the control panel sounded an alarm. Something was rising from the depths below the rig.

The feed started up, and a watery voice filled the room.

"Louis. Louis."

Belinda was alive! I shouted with joy, but again froze as her emotionless, raspy voice continued.

"Meet me in St. Louis, Louis / meet me at the fair / meet me way down theeeeere..."

I scrambled to the floor, searching until I found the toy soldier. I grabbed the toy, the plastic hot and sharp in my fist.

"Send her back!" I cried. "That is my wish!"

***

In a chair across my room, Annie smiles at me as Kayla sits on the floor and continues playing with the toy soldier. Bile rises in my throat. I try desperately to speak, to move my hands, anything to warn them.

"You know, Kayla, your grandpa was a famous marine biologist," Annie says.

"I know," Kayla replies. *Drop the soldier*, I scream, but the scream is only in my mind.

Kayla toddles closer to me, clutching the soldier tight in her fist. "Grandpa, I wish I was just like you."

LOOK TO THE CLASSICS

This story mimics the structure and plot to William Wymark Jacobs' "The Monkey's Paw." First printed in 1902, the story warns of the unintended consequences of wishing literally.

I had entered a flash fiction contest where the prompts I had to write to were horror for the genre and an oil rig for the setting, and a toy soldier had to appear in the story someplace. I would be going up against about twenty-five other writers with the same prompt, and only five of us would advance to the next round of the contest, so I had to come up with something that would appear unique to the judges.

When I'm writing for contests, I usually discard my first five or ten ideas, because if they're obvious to me, they're probably obvious to others, and the more unique stories have a better chance of advancing. So I discarded ideas like aliens coming up from the sea, a haunted oil rig, a toy soldier come to life, and the like.

I then thought about classic stories in the horror genre, starting with Edgar Allen Poe and then moving on to others that I adore, and I thought of "The Monkey's Paw," and it all came together quickly. I added the transfer of the soldier's wishing power to Kayla and having Louis witness it but being unable to stop it as a twist.

Classic stories have become classics for a reason. Hollywood recognizes this (think of how it seems like every movie is a remake, and often not for the better!). Television does too, with franchises, where a hit show spins off a hit show with nearly the same name set in another city, then another city, and so on.

But let's focus on real classic stories. "The Monkey's Paw" is about wish fulfillment—it's akin to the stories of genies granting three wishes. Three really is a magic number in stories. There wouldn't be much of a story if there was one wish granted. Ten would be boring. Three is a great number in storytelling.

In action stories, your character tries and fails; they build up their skills and confidence, and try and fail again; then they realize what they really need to do, and they try for the third time and succeed. In the wishing stories, we make a wish that we think we need, then we scramble to undo that wish because it's not quite right, then we make that third wish and it all goes to pieces (with horror story wishes). In happily-ever-after stories, we learn our lesson and the third wish rights all the wrongs.

Look at a story like Poe's "The Gift of the Magi." It's a simple story on the surface. The husband and wife don't have a lot of money, and they each want to buy the other the perfect gift, so they each sacrifice their most prized possessions in acts of selflessness and love in a classic twist. That's a story that can be rewritten so many ways.

Or Ray Bradbury's "A Sound of Thunder," where a hunter in the past accidentally steps on a butterfly and returns to an Earth drastically altered, showing how small changes can alter the future. That could be rewritten to show how one random event could set off a cascade of unintended consequences in the current day.

There's a fine line between inspiration and blatant rip-off, and I felt like I was in danger of that with this story. There are enough wishing stories that the "The Monkey's Paw" is not unique, plus I had it come from the narrator's POV as Kayla was about to carry on the wishing tradition. Also, W.W. Jacobs' works are in the public domain, as are many classic works, so they really are fair game, although that's not an excuse for me to blatantly rip off a story word for word.

If I were going to emulate that Bradbury story, I wouldn't just write about a time-traveling hunter who steps on a worm instead of a butterfly—I'm not doing anything new, and it wouldn't be a very interesting story anyway since it's already been done. I'd want to use the story as inspiration to push the conceit of small changes affecting the future in a different way —I'd use the story as inspiration.

For your own writing practice, study classic stories for inspiration, then modernize them, extend them, rewrite them from another character's perspective...classic short stories can help get your own creative juices flowing.

And if you want to try rewriting a classic story just for yourself, just for fun, and you don't plan to publish it—then mimic it to your writer's heart's content. Take the whole thing and replace whatever you need to and set in the future, or in the far, far past, or replace all the humans with lemmings and have them speak in Lemmingese (if that's a word). Have fun with it. Just by doing this, you'll learn the structure of the story better than simply reading the story. Again, no publishing your blatant rip-off—this was just for fun—but I'm betting it will spur some creativity and you'll find a way to tweak a classic tale in a way you can publish.

Lesson learned: classic story structures and plots are classics for a reason—use them for inspiration.

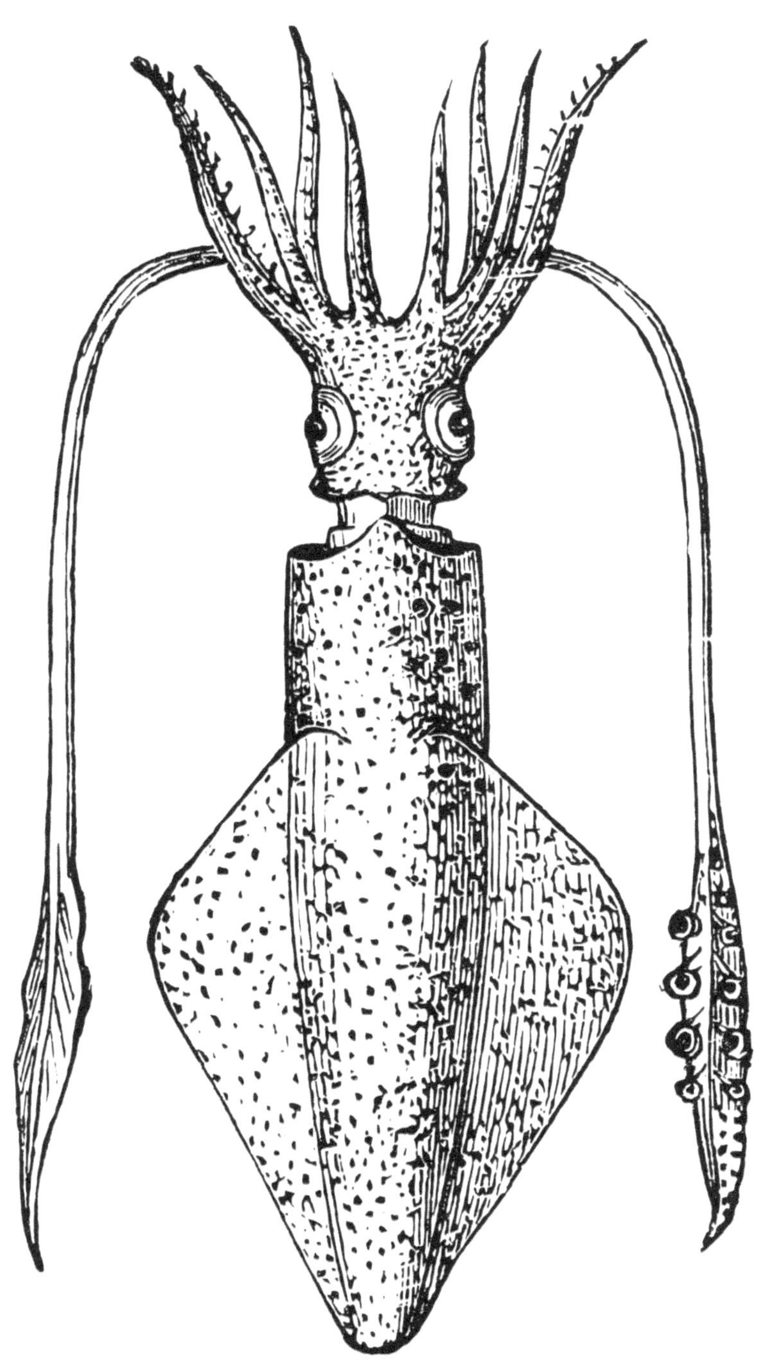

NAILED IT

"Jim," Yvette says to John, "thanks for coming in to interview."

"Thanks for seeing me," John says as he sits. "And it's John."

"John!" Yvette says, laughing. "Sorry. I keep doing that!" She indicates the other two people at the table. "These are my two shift managers, Tish and Octavio." They both nod at John.

The four of them are sitting around a table in Yvette's boutique bakery. It's a Monday, so the bakery is closed. Yvette told John on the phone that she'd be taking today to interview the final candidates for the open baker's job.

"Your resume is solid," Yvette continues, "and so are your references. We need someone pronto, and your skills line up. But this place is a little different from other bakeries, so this in-person interview...it's pretty important. We've been having trouble finding the right person."

John nods, although the place seems to be exactly like the last two bakeries he worked at. Rustic yet cute, and they bake things. It can't be all that different from other bakeries. All he's looking for is a job where he can stay in the back and not deal with anyone.

"Here's the thing," Yvette says, standing and pacing around the table. "Our food is great, we're always busy, we pride ourselves on our exceptional customer service, yada yada. But this part of the city is lousy with boutique bakeries since it was gentrified. I had to set this place apart. I needed…a schtick."

"A schtick?" John asks.

"A schtick," Yvette confirms. "Our schtick is that we slip in double entendres when customers order. And if you know double entendres, you'll know I just said one." Tish and Octavio both nod in agreement.

John goes to say something, but hesitates.

"You look confused," Yvette says, putting her hands on her hips. "Do you even know what a double entendre is?"

"I do," John stammers. Yvette was right. This *is* different. "I just haven't heard of them being applied to selling baked goods." John doesn't consider himself to be that funny a person. He wishes that being snappy with words had been part of the job posting.

Yvette laughs. "A lot of places have schticks. Like those restaurants where the servers act surly on purpose. We even baked the schtick into the name."

"No puns!" Octavio says.

"Sorry," Yvette said. "Octavio's right. I just used a pun, and we don't pun here. Puns are *not* double entendres. Anyway, the schtick is even part of our name." She looks proud.

"The bakery name?" John asks. "Risky?"

"No, not Risky," Yvette says, clucking her tongue in disapproval. She then points to the bakery's name, painted in big block lowercase letters on the wall: rïskäy. "You know. Like risqué."

"I know what risqué means," John says. "But the sign outside says Risky."

"Is that *a* out again?" Tish asks.

Octavio shakes his head. "We need a new neon guy. That umlautted ä sucks."

"You mean *sücks*," Tish says, jabbing two fingers at Octavio to make an air umlaut.

John says, "And this schtick really works? People don't get upset at the double entendres?"

"The old ladies love it," Yvette says, now taking her seat again. "And our customers are ALL old ladies. Well, old or rich. They want to feel cheeky. They want to feel titillated. They want to feel…risqué." She says this last word with a flourish.

This is weird, John thinks. He usually doesn't deal with customers, but he does need a job.

"So let's see if you're rïskäy material, Jim." Yvette then corrects herself. "John. Why do I keep calling him Jim?"

"Because you love to work out, boss. Going hard at the Jim is one of your favorite things," Octavio says. Tish gives him a thumbs up, while Yvette barks out a laugh. John gasps—he's not used to hearing blatant sexual innuendo, especially at work—but the other three act like everything's normal.

"Have we ever had a John work here before?" Yvette asks, stroking her chin. "Wait, no one say anything yet. This is a teachable moment. I'm going to demonstrate how this double entendre thing works."

She turns to Tish and Octavio and repeats the line. "Have we ever had a John work here before?"

"How would we know?" Octavio says. "They're anonymous. They always pay in cash."

"I remember every John I've ever had," Tish purrs.

"I think I get it," John says, now wondering if other bakeries in the city are looking for help.

Yvette smiles. "Great. Let's roleplay. Tish, you be a customer. John, you serve her."

"Really serve her," Octavio starts. "See, that was another—"

Yvette cuts him off. "Let's not overwhelm him."

John gets up and goes around to stand behind the counter. Tish walks up to the counter and holds up a phone charger. She gives him a wink, then says, "Do you know where I can plug this in?"

"There are outlets along the wall," John says.

"No," Yvette says from the table. "No, no, no. Honestly, John, that was a layup."

"Lay up," Octavio says proudly. "And lay down. I'd do either right now."

"See?" Tish asks John, looking disappointed in him. "Like Octavio just did. It's easy."

"Sorry," John says. He feels a little disappointed in himself, too. "I didn't realize we were doing it right away."

Yvette claps her hands twice. "Take two."

Tish looks at John and says, slower this time, "Are the croissants here any good?"

"No, they're the yeast favorite thing we sell," John says. He immediately realizes he's messed up.

"No puns!" Yvette says, shaking her head. John feels himself blush again. "Take three!"

Tish, now speaking to John like he's a toddler, says, "I'm looking for something big enough to feed five people."

"So to speak," John tries.

"We don't do 'so to speak,'" Tish whispers to him. "It's too basic."

John tries again. "That's what she said?"

"No," Yvette says, standing. "No. You aren't Michael Scott. This isn't a fictional paper company. This is a bakery." She sighs and continues. "John, look. No observational ramblings, no anecdotes, no slapstick. And no *The Office* references. I want deadpan, semi-situational, one-liner double entendres. And no puns!" She locks eyes with John. "Focus on the pivot word—a word you can assign multiple meanings to. It'll come."

"Pivot word," John says. "Got it."

This seems ridiculous, he thinks, taking a few deep breaths to ready himself. All he wants to do is bake. He's never been that close with his co-workers before, and he's not sure he wants to start now. Although these people, even though they are pretty twisted, seem nice. Maybe he could make this work.

"Be spontaneous," Yvette adds, sounding a little encouraging. "Be off the cuff."

"Off the cuff," John says. He looks at the rïskäy sign, then at Yvette. How hard can it be to say something that you normally wouldn't say? How hard can it be to be someone other than yourself?

He has an idea. "Do you have any suggestions for getting it off the cuff? I've got some there AND on my collar. It was quite the night."

The other three burst out laughing. Tish high-fives him and says, "Nailed it!"

"Nice, new guy!" Octavio says.

"Really?" John asks. He feels oddly proud.

"Yes," Yvette says, beaming. She walks over to shake John's hand. "Welcome to rïskäy."

LEARN YOUR SUPERPOWERS

I'd been busy editing client manuscripts and hadn't done much creative writing, so I wanted to take a few hours to spend on a short story. I've taken enough of these needed creativity breaks that I didn't need to spend much time deciding what type of story to write—I lean on my creative superpower, which is writing something light and silly. This story came together in a few hours and I got the outlet I needed, then it was back to the client work.

It's great to push ourselves to try new genres and new styles. But sometimes it's great to lean on what we know when we just need to write. If you know that the easiest type of story for you to start is a romance, and all you want to do is write, then write some romance scenes. If it's a lengthy hand-to-hand battle scene that will get you writing, then write that. For me, it's something light with a weird premise, like this.

I've talked a little about contests. Here are how some of them work and how you leaning on your superpower can come in handy.

A contest might give you five days to write and submit a 1,500-word short story. You might be assigned the genre, the setting, a main character, and/or an object that has to appear in the story.

For example, you might get action/adventure as the genre, a banker as the main character, and an abandoned factory as the setting (the prompts can be that random!).

If you love writing hand-to-hand combat stories, then your 1,500-w0rd story might be full of action (although it still has to have an opening, a middle, an ending, a structure—all the stuff that makes a story a story). For the contest, the banker might have to fight their way out of an abandoned factory. It fits with the given genre. As long as you can come up with a full story (why is the banker there?), it works. Or maybe the banker is one of the fighters preventing someone from escaping the factory?

For me, if I were stuck on that prompt, I might turn to my "superpower"—silly premise—and think how to add that to my contest prompts. Maybe the banker defeats their foes accidentally throughout the story. Like they trip over something and it just happens to release a plume of fire prevention chemicals that masks their escape. That story would probably be as light in tone as "Nailed It" is. As long as I had action and adventure in there as the main genre, I could also add comedy and lightness, and the story would probably stick out from the other stories, which would probably focus more on serious action.

After you write a lot of short stories and scenes for practice and submission, you'll have a sense for the style and tone and genre for the writing that comes easier for you. You might consider those your superpowers. Writing in first person instead of third person, or writing in present tense instead of past, or writing with a lot of dialogue or none at all, might be superpowers as well.

I know some writers who write in several genres, but they can write steamy romance that is so steamy that it can strip the paint off the walls, and do so without giving it a second thought. That's their superpower, the type of writing they turn to when they want to just write. Other writers like to write those hand-to-hand battle scenes for practice—give them two characters, two random weapons, and a random setting, and in thirty minutes, they'll churn out an incredibly well-written battle scene.

Besides the silly stuff, I'll warm up by writing dialogue between two characters I make up on the fly—one character will say something, then I'll make up the response, and back and forth and back and forth. That helps me prep for the times when I need to write quick, snappy dialogue for a book or story, because I don't need exercise that writing muscle for as long—my dialogue won't feel forced or unnatural because I've already given that writing muscle a lot of working out.

Remember your superpowers so that when you need to write a story quickly, or when you need to write just to write for an outlet or for play, you can draw on those powers to start writing faster and easier. Those superpowers also come in handy when you are writing a novel, because if that novel touches on the tone or genre of your superpower writing, you'll find that the words fly.

Lesson learned: when you need to write quickly, or want to write for fun, lean on what you write well.

HAVE A CIGAR

You: Where am I?

Gravelly Voice: Hey, New Guy's awake.

High Voice: And now there are four of us.

You: Who's there? Who's talking?

Slow Voice: You're in a—

You: What's around my legs? Why is it so dark?

High: Typical New Guy questions. It's dark because there's no light. As for what's around your legs…

Gravel: Don't bother struggling, pal. You can't get free. And neither can we. We've tried everything. You're stuck down here like the rest of us.

You: Hey! Help! Get me out of here!

High: Stop screaming, New Guy! You're breaking the mood. Although I will admit that I screamed the same thing when I woke up shackled.

Gravel: No one's coming for you, sweetheart. No one can hear you.

Slow: Except us, because we're all locked up down—

You: I don't understand. Who are you people? Where am I?

High: Where are WE. A basement. We think. Or a cold, pitch-black penthouse with a terrible view.

You: Why? Why are we here?

Gravel: We don't know.

Slow: It's been days since—

High: Has it?

Slow: It feels like days to me, because I remember—

High: You know how it is on vacation. You lose track of time.

Gravel: Sadistic assholes, whoever did this to us.

You: I don't understand. What's happening?

High: First rule of Kidnap Club: not understanding Kidnap Club.

Gravel: Look, you being New Guy, we'll save you some time. We're each sitting on a metal chair. We're cuffed by our legs to the chair, which is bolted to the floor. Our hands are free, but that does us no good. We're facing each other in a circle, we think, but we can't touch each other. We think we're in a basement. There's no light, obviously. None of us can see a thing. We don't know each other. We don't know how long we've been here. We don't know why we're here. We don't know who did this to us.

You: I was at my place, someone knocked on the door...I opened the door...someone was...I don't remember anything after that. What did they do to me?

Slow: Same they did to all of us, we were all—

Gravel: They drugged us. Took us here. Locked us up.

You: Where is here? Who are they? Who are you people? How did I get here?

Gravel: They carried you down here. Same as they did to us, we think.

High: A shared experience among friends. At least we have that in common.

Slow: They told us not to say anything when they're down here or they'd hit us with—

Gravel: Felt like a wrench to me.

High: You shouldn't have said anything. Then they wouldn't have hit you. You didn't see *me* talking. Wait. You didn't *hear* me talking. I'm losing my edge, people!

Gravel: Funny guy, aren't you? Well, I'm not taking this lying down, asshole.

High: Wish I *could* lie down. This vacation sucks. I'm definitely complaining to management. Zero stars, would not recommend.

You: None of this makes sense.

Gravel: Look, New Guy, you can't fight them, you can't escape, you can't leave. We tried everything already. I'm just saving you time.

Slow: We tried to—

High: Welcome to the party, pal.

You: And you guys don't know each other? You have no idea why you're here?

Gravel: No idea.

You: And no idea where you are?

Slow: A basement, probably in a house, sometimes it sounds like—

Gravel: Sometimes we hear them walking around up there. Upstairs. They're gonna pay for this when I get out. You'll see.

You: It smells terrible in here.

Slow: There are buckets under the chairs for—

Gravel: Under your chair is a bucket if you need to piss or shit. Drag it out with your hands. But put it back under your chair so you don't knock it over when you're done. We learned that the hard way.

Slow: Sorry about that, I didn't mean to—

High: There's something else. Another smell. Something sour. It's gotten worse since I got here. It's not me, though.

Slow: I work at the cannery, second shift, that smells like something's—

Gravel: Fuck the cannery.

High: Why fuck the cannery?

Gravel: Because the guy who runs the cannery is an asshole.

High: Why is he an asshole?

Gravel: Why is anyone an asshole?

High: Wait, he works at the cannery, and you know the guy who runs the cannery?

Gravel: So what? Small town, right?

High: You know a lot of guys.

Gravel: I know as many guys as I need to know.

High: Maybe that's it. Maybe this is about the cannery.

Gravel: Maybe one of you assholes knows more than you think.

Slow: I don't recognize anyone's—

Gravel: You said you work second shift. You can't know everyone.

Slow: But I've worked there for eight years, since—

Gravel: This has gotta be about the cannery. But nah, this can't be about the cannery.

High: Guess the cannery was a red herring. Get it? Herring? Cannery? I still got it!

Slow: I've been straight for eight years, got a girl, got a place, got a job at the cannery, I'm not involved in anything bad anymore, I keep my head down and my nose—

Gravel: Well, fuck the guy at the cannery anyway, but maybe it is just coincidence. Maybe you've got some new info, New Guy. Let's see what you remember. Take us through it.

You: Take you through what?

High: How you got here. What you remember. How they got you.

You: Like I said, it was a guy, or maybe two…it was quick, I opened the door, stepped back…then I don't remember anything, just waking up here.

Gravel: You remember anything about the guys? White, brown, black, big, little?

You: Nothing. What do you guys remember?

Slow: I go to work, I go home after shift, I don't take the bus, I need to save the money, it's not a long walk, then somebody bumps me from behind, I hadn't heard anybody coming, then—

Gravel: I don't remember anything at all, really. I was in my car, pulled over off Fernwood. You know that pullout? I closed my eyes, had a long day, then I'm here. They must have sprayed me with something, I had the windows down, but shit, I don't remember anything except flashes of me flailing around. Then I woke up here, I was the first, I had no idea what was happening. No idea how long. My fucking ankle is still bleeding, I think. I fought against these shackles like a trapped animal.

High: Which you smell like, by the way. A wild animal.

Gravel: Fuck you.

High: I was in my house. My own house. My girlfriend and her kids are sleeping, I hear a noise, sounded like a cat but I don't have a cat, it's the middle of the night, I start walking around, and bam, I get hit, but I don't know with what.

You: Hit where? Hit with what?

High: I dunno. Like I remember getting hit, but I don't remember where. Maybe the nose? I don't know. You can't put a guy down by just hitting them in the nose, can you?

Gravel: Then one by one we wake up here, like we're in a fucking zoo.

High: A zoo without customers. Or lights. Or cotton candy.

Gravel: Fuck you again, funny guy.

Slow: That smell is getting—

Gravel: I don't smell shit.

High: I *do* smell shit. Oh right, because there's a bucket of shit under my chair.

Slow: It smells sour, like—

Gravel: Quiet! Listen. They're walking around up there.

High: That's nothing.

Slow: I don't hear—

Gravel: That's them. The bastards that did this to us.

You: Do they ever come down here?

Slow: Just when they bring someone new down—

High: I'm starving. I need water. The service in this place is terrible. I'm definitely giving them that bad Yelp.

Slow: Cigars, I smelled cigars when—

Gravel: The fuck?

High: Do you shit cigars? Because over here, it still smells like shit, not cigars.

Slow: No, cigars, I remember now, I smelled a cigar, in the car, however they took us here, I woke up for a second or two, I think, I remember smelling a cigar in the—

Gravel: In their car?

You: Concentrate on the smell. Smell can be a powerful trigger.

High: La di da, I guess the brainiac cracked the case wide open. Although come to think of it...did I smell a cigar when they took me?

Gravel: Shut the fuck up. Give me a minute. Something. Cigars. Who smoked them a lot? Why is that familiar?

Slow: I used to do work for a guy who—

Gravel: Oh no. It can't be the same guy. It can't be him.

High: What are you two dipwads talking about?

Gravel: I don't want to say his name. In case he's listening.

High: Who's listening? Whoever took us? They know who we are. They kidnapped us, remember? If he's listening, then he definitely knows who we are.

Slow: If it's the guy I'm thinking—

Gravel: Mooney.

High: Mooney? Oh, Mooney. Shit.

Slow: That's who I was thinking of, Mooney, he's the guy I used to—

Gravel: Knew him back then. He had this thing about cigars. He loved the smell of them. Every place he had was fucking soaked in the smell of cigars. Swear he used to light them and not smoke them just for the smell.

Slow: I haven't seen Mooney in eight years ago, since—

High: Wait, we all know Mooney? How is that possible?

Gravel: It's gotta be eight years for me too.

High: I haven't seen him since...I'd rather not say.

Gravel: We can't talk about this here.

Slow: If it's Mooney, he already knows about us, but if it isn't, it doesn't—

High: That's gotta be it, right? The connection? But why? Why Mooney? After all this time?

You: Maybe if you guys said how you knew Mooney, you'd figure out the connection.

Gravel: Do you know Mooney, New Guy?

You: I really can't say.

High: That's gotta be it. It's gotta be Mooney.

You: When was the last time any of you saw this Mooney?

Gravel: It's gotta be, like I said, eight years?

Slow: It's been eight years for me, I know that exactly, I got out of the business right after the night when—

High: I did something for Mooney eight years ago, but it wasn't at night. That much I remember. No way could I ever forget it.

Gravel: If you mean the same night as I'm thinking, then that could be it. It's gotta be it.

Slow: So why would Mooney—

Gravel: I don't want to think about it if it is him. That's why I left. Years ago. I got far away. If we're here...but this can't be Mooney's place, right? Is that where we are?

Slow: Talking about it is the only way we'll ever figure out if—

Gravel: I'm not implicating myself here.

High: How the fuck can you implement yourself? If Mooney took us, then he already knows what you did, whatever the fuck that was. I meant implicate. Just repeat all of what I said but say implicate instead of implement.

Gravel: That's the thing. The last time I saw Mooney...did any work for him...I didn't do anything wrong. I mean, Mooney was bat-shit crazy. Fugazi in the head.

Slow: After what I did, I got out of the business, I cleaned myself up, started working at the cannery, got a girl and a—

High: I mean, if this is about what I think you're talking about...but why would Mooney bring us all here? I haven't done that kind of work again since. After that last job, I just couldn't. I mean, I'm not saying that you guys did the same work, I don't know what you did. Although I'm betting you didn't do what I did.

Slow: Are we even talking about the same—

Gravel: Fucking Mooney. It has to be.

High: So what did you do?

Slow: I'm gonna be sick if this is about—

High: Use your cigar-scented bucket if you get sick. But don't kick it over again. You'll ruin the floor.

Gravel: Shut up! All of you! This can't be…can it?

High: Maybe he just wants us to confess our sins to each other. Maybe that's why we're here. I'll talk if it means I don't have to die.

Gravel: Mooney doesn't care about sins. He paid me, us, to do…whatever he needed.

Slow: That last job—

High: I've done some crazy shit, but what he had me do that time…

Slow: I think we need to say what we did, if this is about Mooney, because it's the only way we'll—

Gravel: I ran.

High: You ran?

Gravel: That night. If we're talking about the same night…I guess it doesn't matter at this point if he's listening or not. Here's what happened. Mooney asked me to help him, said this guy was going to show up, some guy who Mooney thought had crossed him or some shit, I don't know, didn't care, he wanted me there in case things went sideways. I used to do that stuff… but I never did anything like that night before.

High: So what happened?

Gravel: This guy shows up, he's a little guy, short, you know? And he's got this woman with him, really pretty, dark hair, and she's smiling like she doesn't know what's going on at all, like they're on a fucking date or something, pretty thing, gap between her front teeth, it was sexy, not sure why I remembered it, I only saw her for a minute. She was the kind of girl a guy like me could never have.

High: Oh fuck. The gap-toothed girl. It's the same girl.

Gravel: You know that girl?

High: I said I don't want to talk about it yet.

Slow: I don't know anything about a girl, but I do know about a short—

Gravel: So Mooney and the guy get into it, the girl doesn't know what's happening, and the little guy, he's up in Mooney's face, and Mooney yells at me to help, but I don't what I'm supposed to do, it's crazy, everything is happening at once, and Mooney grabs this bat, baseball bat, aluminum, he always kept it by his door, and he whacks the guy in the head, and the guy drops. Dead. Everything goes quiet, then Mooney, he takes the girl, wrestles her down, she's screaming now, and I, I heard him, what he did to her...And I took off. I never looked back. I got far away from there, I wanted no part, I could have saved her...I don't know what happened after that.

High: I didn't know about the guy. But I do know about the girl.

Slow: I don't know anything about the girl, but I do know about the little—

High: Mooney had me...see, I owed Mooney a lot, I mean, a *lot* of money. So he called me, asked me, told me he had something he needed me to do. You gotta understand, I had no way out, there was no other way for me to get out from under this...So I get to Mooney's place, and he shows me the girl. She's dead. Been dead for, I don't know, a while. Mooney points me to a power saw and says, "Get rid of her." Which I did. It was...horriblic. Horrific.

Gravel: And it's the same girl.

High: Gap-tooth girl, pretty. I tried to put that day behind me, but her face...I see that face in every nightmare, and I have a nightmare every night.

Gravel: If I had stayed, I could have saved her. If I hadn't run...

Slow: I never saw the girl, don't know anything about a girl, but Mooney had a hold over me too, actually over my sister, and Mooney calls her to call me, says he has something that will get my sister out of his debt, family, you have to help family, so I go there, and Mooney shows me the guy, that little guy, says he's dead, get rid of him, and if he's not dead, make him dead, and I don't know if the guy is dead, so I say I'll take care of it, I had to, it was for my sister, and—

High: This is the longest non-story in the history of mankind. Can you get to the point?

Slow: I take the guy, drive the body, the guy, far away, but I can't bury the guy, and I can't kill him, I just can't do any of it, so I leave him in the woods, I don't know if he's dead or not, and Mooney wants me to go back and clean up the place, and that will pay my sister's debt, so I go back, get rid of everything, and just like that, my sister, she's free, don't you understand, she's free from Mooney, and I left, I cleaned up, and now I got a girl, got a place, got a job at the cannery, I don't know what happened after that, I never asked, I never—

Gravel: So that's it. This is all about Mooney. But why now? That was eight years ago. And we all did what he asked us to do. So what is he doing to us now?

Slow: That smell is definitely getting worse. What is that—

You: That's Mooney.

Gravel: What's Mooney?

You: The smell. Mooney's in the corner. Dead. I bashed in his skull, just like he bashed in mine. Only I did a better job than he did. Obviously.

Gravel: You're...the little guy?

You: It took forever to learn to walk again. It took forever to find Lissie's body...and it took forever to track down Mooney. But it *didn't* take forever for him to tell me who helped him eight years ago. So I tracked down the three of you and brought you here. To learn who knew what. To learn who *did* what.

High: You gotta believe me, I didn't know—

You: You know exactly what you did to her.

Gravel: I didn't do—

You: That's the problem. You didn't do *anything*. You didn't *stop* anything. And she's dead because of you.

Slow: I didn't know anything—

You: You're right. You didn't know. So I'll let you go.

High: Is Lissie the name of the girl who's been haunting—

Gravel: Look, buddy, I know better now, I should have—

Slow: I'm so sorry that I left you.

You: Like I said, I'm going to let you go. After.

Slow: After what?

You: After you kill the other two with a baseball bat. And then cut up their bodies, and Mooney's, with a power saw.

KNOW YOUR NARRATOR'S ROLE

"Have A Cigar" is an extreme example of a narrator's limited role. Here, the narrator relays only the dialogue, and does so in script form. When I thought up this story, I made the decision to not have a traditional narrator, but I also didn't want any of the characters to take on the role of a false narrator and say anything that sounded strained and unnatural, like "As you know, we are in a basement that is totally dark, it's about twenty feet by twenty feet with no windows..." . The information about setting and situation had to come solely through dialogue that sounded authentic.

I tried to bolster the story by giving the three people who aren't "You" their own distinct voices. "Slow" never gets to finish a sentence until the end—all of his dialogue is cut off by the "High" and "Gravel." "High" is bitterly sarcastic throughout (and comes across as a pain in the ass), while "Gravel" has the classic "tough guy" speech pattern and know-it-all attitude. As the story goes on, "You" stop talking and let the three take over while "You" listens.

A classic fairy-tale opening is "Once upon a time...", which indicates right away that it's being told by a narrator. Stories told in the first person point of view (told by "I") are narrated by that character, who describes what is happening as well as letting us into their head.

Third-person stories (not "I went to lunch" but "Dave went to lunch") have narrators as well, and this is where authors have to find the balance between how much of the story the narrator tells and how much the character tells—how deep and how often we are in the characters' heads, how often information is relayed through dialogue and action instead of the narrator summarizing the story, and much more. "Have a Cigar" is written in the third person—imagine the narrator is also in that basement. We are not in any one character's head. The narrator is recording only the dialogue and noting who spoke it, and that is it; the story is just a transcription of what was spoken.

A "rule" that writers come across all the time is "Show, don't tell"—meaning don't have the narrator do all the storytelling, but have the characters "show" the story. It's a true rule, but it's also not true. There are very good reasons for having "tell" in your story. For instance, if "Dave" walks into a crumbling cabin as he's searching for a lost child, it'd probably sound false to the reader if Dave speaks aloud to no one, "Hmm. Decrepit boards, the smell of mold, pools of water—this place looks unsafe." Dave can think it if the author has already established that descriptions are coming from Dave's point of view. Otherwise, it's a good choice to have the narrator "tell" us what the scene looks like.

If you look back at the previous story, "Nailed It," there's this line:

"Here's the thing," Yvette says, standing and pacing around the table.

That last part, standing and pacing around the table, is from the narrator. That story is written in third person ("John" instead of "I"), and although we do get into John's head and listen in on some of his thoughts and see what he sees, it's not all the time. The narrator describes the action of Yvette moving around and records what she says.

The narrator also relays a lot of the story even though we are in John's head:

"A schtick?" John asks.

The narrator is telling us what John says even though John is the story's point of view character. The narrator is watching everyone and listening to everyone talk, even John. That's because I wrote this in third person—a "third person" is always in the room, recording what is happening.

It's important to have a strategy for how you will use the narrator in your writing, from novels all the way down to flash fiction. "Have A Cigar" is, again, an extreme example—it's all dialogue, and after a few drafts, I eliminated all traces of the narrator except for the transcription.

In "Nailed It," the narrator is perched on John's shoulder, seeing what he sees and listening in to his thoughts, but is not walking around the room, going outside while the characters are talking, or listening in to other characters' thoughts. The narrator can observe John if needed, or dive into John's head at any time. I "limited" the narrator to getting into just John's head. This is called "third person limited" point of view, limiting the point of view to one perspective.

One of the best ways to learn about how to best choose what

your narrator should do for your story is read a lot. The trickiest POV is usually how "close" to get in third person, but there are millions of books written in third person. I'm an advocate for reading little-known authors and independently-published authors, but if you're looking to study POV, there's no better way than to read widely-known best-selling authors in a variety of genres (think any author whose books you can buy in an airport) and see how they handle balancing their third-person POV characters' actions and inner thoughts, especially when they switch to a different POV character in each chapter. Read these books for fun, but also study them mechanically. How often do they use "she thought?" when the character is clearly thinking about something? How often does the narrator interpret the action or the setting instead of the character doing so? Established, best-selling authors find the right balance for these and other questions really well, then keep everything consistent throughout the novel so that the narrator's role becomes invisible instead of jarring.

It takes a lot of work, meaning it takes a lot of writing that you'll discard over time, but taking charge of your narrator's role will strengthen your characters.

Lesson learned: every story has a narrator—define their role early for consistency.

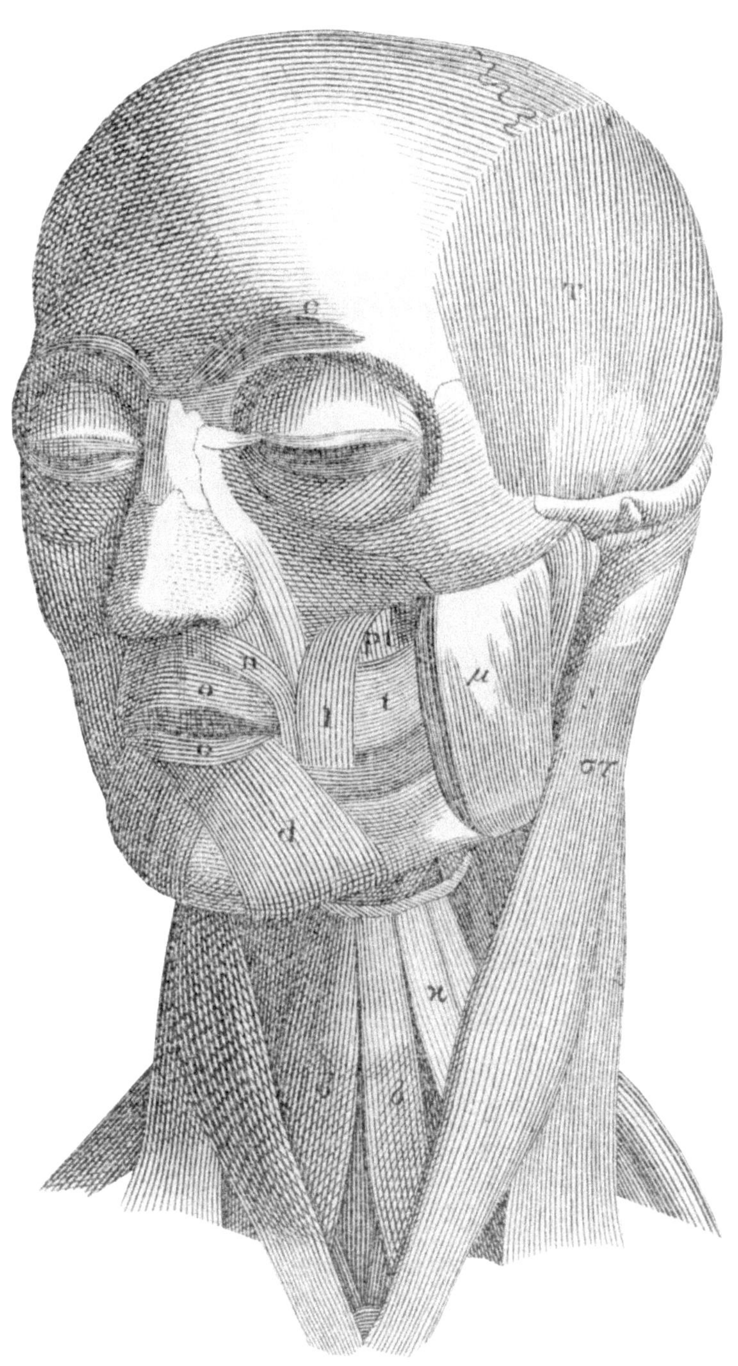

CHAOS

You watch the three main players in tonight's drama with delight as your urge to feed on the chaos yet to come grows stronger. And how could it not? Chaos is your ambrosia.

The first player is the thief. Whether they stole out of spite, need, or boredom matters not to you. They set all this in motion. And they will get away with it. How happy you are that they set all this in motion. How delicious will be the chaos that ensues.

The second player is Elinor Lynch, the grande dame of the Marketing team and hostess of today's annual Holiday Open House, held here in her festively bedecked three-story brownstone in the best part of Boston. You have seen her work, you have seen her play, and you know that in all that she does, Elinor craves power, respect, and authority. How happy you will be to see her lose the respect of everyone here, to see her fall from faux grace, to see her unearned privilege devastated. How you anticipate the ruin that will follow in her wake.

The third player is Nadia Correa, fill-in caterer, who three days earlier received a call from a suddenly-sick competitor begging her to take this one job for her, to not leave the client in the lurch. Nadia desperately needed the work. And she pulled it off. What happens here tonight is no indictment of Nadia's canapés or curried chicken on little wooden spears. You have watched Nadia labor hard tonight, dealing with trays, napkins, small plates, plastic cups, entitled guests, an overly long toast, a hot oven, a cramped kitchen, no help, and impeccable timing, doing everything herself to save money and maximize profit. You have seen how frazzled the last three days have been for Nadia, a hurried meeting with Elinor to learn the arrangements, the shopping, the planning, her first job in this part of town, a light end to a dark year, a needed job, the potential to make a name for herself, desperate to become who she hoped to be with hard work and the right break.

The other thirty-odd guests, none of whom need names, include a few folk from the neighborhood, their dragged-along spouses, and fellow workers under and alongside Elinor in Marketing. One of them is the thief. For all in attendance, the party feels not a celebration, but a millstone, an obligation, a date circled on the calendar with hope that illness, weather, or a minor accident would postpone their presence.

The party started ninety minutes ago. There is laughter, joy, merriment—some of it real, much of it faked. But you do not care about joy and merriment. You came here to feed.

You scan the room to get a better sense of the supporting cast to learn what they brought and what they have left behind. No matter what course their lives have taken, all of their paths led to them being here, in this moment, in this place, the intersection of Fate and Determinism with Free Will and Randomness. For nearly all of the guests, it will be the last time they step foot in this brownstone, yet none of them yet know it. You stifle a giggle and feel the hunger pangs.

There! A man afraid to speak his mind in front of his wife,

whose hand he clenches too weakly in public and too firmly in private.

There! Elinor's best friend, but put that phrase in quotes, as she doesn't like Elinor all that much and is more about the game, the deception, drawn to drama like a toad to fat flies. It would be easy to assume that she is the thief, but you know that she is not. She is here hoping that for once, something dramatic will happen. For once, she will not be disappointed.

There! Elinor's work underlings, a knot of them, all much younger than her, huddled in a corner, taking over a couch, dressed in their best merry merry ho ho, hostess gifts delicately placed one next to the other on a side table, shoes and boots stomped thoughtfully to rid them of snow, a Saturday night sacrificed for the betterment of their careers as they gossip about Elinor.

There! The thief.

You watch the guests mingle, the smell of something tantalizing coming from the kitchen, the aroma of food mixed with impending chaos, and you watch the players find their places, Elinor circulating through the room like a feather carried on a breeze, over here to say hello and thank you so much for coming, then there to partake in some idle chatter and forced laughter. You watch Nadia make a pass through the room with wine, and you watch the thief try to appear nonchalant, then you turn back to watch Elinor continue across the room, and wasn't it a great year for us all, then she turns toward the fireplace.

Finally.

The lack of something on the mantel catches her eye but she doesn't yet process it, she can't yet see what isn't there, and at this you stifle another giggle and feel the ache, the throb.

Drinks flow, food is eaten, and contemporary jazz, barely audible, emanates from speakers masked as nutcrackers artfully placed throughout the home. Now Nadia passes hors d'oeuvres, forcing a smile, tamping down her nerves, thinking to herself that she has pulled this off, while the underlings and the dragged-along spouses check their watches and phones, their appearances now made, wondering as all party guests do just how long one must stay to have been noted as attending.

Elinor flits from grouping to grouping, and here you hold your breath with anticipation, but you want to shriek with delight as her gaze flicks to the mantel again, and this time she processes it, this time she sees what is not there.

—My bird! Elinor shouts. —My bird is gone!

The bird in question is a black opal sculpture, sized to rest in a palm for easy display or clenched in a fist and thrust deep into a pocket—as was done by the thief—its weight 110.7 carats, finished into a bird of indeterminate species. It is beautiful in the dark way that black opal is both stunning and sad. You watched the thief take it earlier, a quick snatch, a heist hard to pull off in a venue this small and crowded, so many lights chasing away the shadows where one would normally hide, so many pairs of eyes to spot the pull.

You wonder for a moment about Elinor's lack of tact and graciousness here. Would it not have been better for Elinor to take note silently rather than erupt, as she soon will? Would it have been better to ponder the mystery later than to immediately accuse? Of course it would have been, although better is relative, as you adore, need, the chaos to come. It would have been better for everyone else had Elinor held her tongue, as fewer lives would be decimated, but worse for you— meaning things turned out perfectly.

—My bird is gone! Elinor repeats. —Has anyone seen it? Elinor then launches into a description, one not worth transcribing, a rambling far too long and descriptive, as if the piece could easily be confused with other black opal pieces strewn about the brownstone, as if the guests perhaps had brought their own opal bird carvings, ones easily confused with the piece purloined.

No one answers in the affirmative, of course. Only the thief knows where the bird is, and the thief isn't saying anything. And here is where Things Get Interesting.

—No one is leaving here until I find my bird! spits Elinor Lynch, and at this you shake unseen with glee and mirth, for this is why you came, this moment and the larger one that will soon follow, and later to see the worm turn, only that will be weeks from now, but this moment is blissfully chaotic in itself, so you feed off this initial wave of chaos, and it is so, so delicious.

Elinor's last utterance stuns the room into silence, and even the nutcracker speakers seem to fall mute in shock, although loud proclamations like this from Elinor do not come as a complete surprise to those gathered here. Those who work under Elinor see such outbursts regularly, as Marketing is nothing if not a stressful division and Elinor is the cause of most of that stress. Of the neighbors, some have suspected Elinor to have a frail ego clad in marble, while others have witnessed it firsthand. —Keep the music down! —Who didn't clean up their dog shit? —This neighborhood is changing!

And here you pause. You don't know Elinor's real reason for dealing with this now, for wanting the party to stop to find justice, if justice is even to be found, and in this fashion, rather than waiting with discretion. Did she have a bad day, a bad week, a bad life? Was a last straw placed on the back of the metaphorical camel? The opal bird was expensive and unique, but was there sentimentality attached to it? In Elinor's ramblings, the piece seems lathered in sentimentality, but you know that's not true. She bought the piece merely for show, she hoped beyond hope that someone tonight would ask about it so she could casually exclaim, —Oh, that? Well, there's a story there...

Also, you don't care about Elinor's reason for her outburst. You don't care about what would have been "better" or less reprehensible. The guests will care, of course; in fact, the echoes from this outburst and what is yet to come will reverberate around the brownstone, and Marketing, and many other places, for months.

The chaos she created and is about to create is what you seek.

You examine the subtle currents, sniff out how the room has changed in the last few seconds. For the guests who are readers, the scene takes on the feel of an Agatha Christie novel, while to those embracing recent film, it is more *Knives Out*. For Nadia, these currents mirror real life, her life, because young, brown-skinned women in this wealthy, white-skinned neighborhood are always among the first to get the side-eye, the tongue-wag, the refusal of the benefit of doubt.

You ponder the crime. Later, after Nadia leaves in tears and many of the guests storm out in disgust and shock, there will be a search, but a fruitless one. At present, no one has left this level of the brownstone, save the smokers, banished to the rooftop deck to inhale and exhale, and you already know that the purloined object is not on the roof, it wasn't dropped over the side for later retrieval. It is here, in this room, stashed in a pocket not six feet from the mantel, the thrill of the grift still coursing through the thief's system like the rush of nicotine, the pleasure centers in their brain still firing wildly because they got away with it.

You circulate unseen throughout the room to listen to the whispers before the accusation to come. —A theft? Here?—It's misplaced. —Did you hear what she said? —What's she going on about? —What's this about a bird? —Are her parties always like this? —How can you stand working for her? One of those was uttered by the thief, and that causes you to stifle yet another giggle. You and they are kindred spirits, in a fashion, although you are ethereal, not mortal and corporeal.

You think about the thief's motives as you brush by them unseen, their drink in hand as they pretend to act as dumbfounded as the innocents. Have they done this before? Was the theft planned, or a momentary spur? Would their answers heighten the crime, or lessen it, in the eyes of the others, should their motives be known? But there is no time or need to rewind into the thief's life to examine their Dickensian. They did what they did, and the ripples of their act will soon allow you to gorge.

The theft is a crime, but the real crime, although not a violation of the law, is the withered, privileged finger about to point. If you could salivate, right now you would, because that first wave of chaos did not sate you. It drove your hunger even higher.

You do not care who stole what or who gets away with what, but you do seek to understand how this evening will change everyone going forward, and to better understand the impacts— lost respect, newfound courage, one marriage ruined. It will help you, going forward, to better gauge how much chaos can erupt from someone saying just three simple words.

Besides, you are not here to witness the solution to a mystery. This is no Christie closed-room whodunit, but a snapshot into power and who can wield it, and what power even is, how fleeting, the power to accuse without reciprocity, and the power to steal, to covet, and how power feels once unleashed, and how all that power creates chaos, and what it feels like when power comes crashing down upon you and you are powerless to prevent it.

The guests continue their silence as they, and you, watch

Elinor take in the room, watch her pin each guest with her eyes, and you wonder what she is thinking when her gaze alights on each, but you wonder no more when her gaze finds Nadia, as you knew it would.

Elinor, her face both reddening and blanching, a difficult thing to accomplish, a decision made, because Elinor is always right even when she is wrong, strides across the room and stops in front of Nadia, who has been frozen, half in the kitchen, half out, a tray of stuffed mushrooms still balanced in one hand, watching, listening, hoping against all hope that she won't be dragged into whatever is happening, suddenly ruing having taken this job, feeling the all too familiar cloak of guilt by class and color draped around her even though she has nothing to feel guilty about for she is of course not the thief, feeling small, feeling a buzzing deep in her head, an alarm, a warning, a plea to run from those who wield power and class against you, the urge to run ratcheted ten-fold when Elinor's eyes meet hers and when Elinor approaches her.

This, this is the moment you have craved, The Moment Where Everything Will Change. You watch Elinor open her mouth, and your lust for chaos is nearly a frenzy, for finally, it is Time.

—Open your bag! Elinor yells at Nadia.

Yes! you cry out, although no one can hear you, and you feed, feed, feed on the chaos of a baseless accusation and the reactions, the shouts, the anger, the tears. The chaos.

This is a tiny event in scope. Zoom out, and quickly this brownstone, this city, all but disappear, a speck amongst many other specks. This gathering turned allegation will be an event that none in attendance will ever forget, and it will forever alter the course of both Elinor and Nadia, but for nearly everyone else on the planet, this event is a non-event. The world will continue to turn.

And that is one of the wonders, or horrors, of being human, you have learned. That no matter the best day of their lives, or the worst, the world really does not care what happens to them. What is monumental to them, what is life-changing, is nothing to the rest of humanity. The world is too big, and they are too small. How small their problems really are, you think. How little they matter.

But still, no one here will ever forget how they felt when Elinor accused Nadia because she was The Other. And you will never forget that eruption of chaos, and how it tasted, and how you could feed on it for days and never feel full.

GET OUT OF YOUR COMFORT ZONE

I didn't like writing this story, I didn't like editing this story, I still don't like reading this story, and I'm uncomfortable that this story is nestled amongst the other stories. But, that's why I wrote it, and that's why I'm including it.

The prose is too rich. The main character is too vague—is it a demon? But that character also knows that Elinor's awful spoken line is coming, so has it been here before? Is the character an invisible time-traveling demon who's seen this happen before and has returned to feed again on the chaos?

The only reason I wrote this story is because I had a clear picture of the room and the party being set up; then I had a clear picture of Elinor strutting about and basking in her power; then I had a clear picture of Nadia as The Other; and then I "heard" demonic laughter. Then I started writing, with no idea about the plot, and eventually this came out.

I like to stay with the familiar. I like to write what I like to write. Simple, direct prose. But I put this in front of my critique groups, and it prompted a lot of discussion, much of it way above my head, because my critique group partners are very deep thinkers, so I went back to the story even though I wanted to lob it in the back of my writing closet and continued to revise it, and even now I don't know how I feel about it. But I'm including it as a reminder that even though I just talked about superpowers and going to them when you want to write, sometimes ideas come up that force us to be uncomfortable.

For me, it wasn't the subject matter; it was the way the words were coming out. I tried to shape the story a different way, but it was like the words kept coming out *another* way, forcing themselves to into a complex and peculiar style. The narrator here, the "you," took over the story, speaking in its own fashion, using language in ways I don't normally use, forcing me to keep up instead of being in control of the writing

Writing is…odd. I'll coach my clients that *we* are the gods and goddesses, that *we* control our characters on the page, that *we* build the worlds and create our characters out of nothing. *We* are the bosses. If a story isn't working, *we* hold the power. If the words aren't working, *we* can replace them without consequence. As an editor, it's my job to step in when my clients are unable or unwilling to take control.

And yet…sometimes I'm not in control. Sometimes I don't want to touch certain stories after I finish them. They make me feel uncomfortable. Sometimes as writers, we give birth to stories that are good enough to keep, but we really disliked the process.

Non-writers: that may sound like so much b*llshit, I know. But it's true. Sometimes we writers are like the two travelers in *An American Werewolf in London* and the truck driver says to us, "Keep off the moors and stick to the roads," and sure, we could pester him for an explanation…or we can accept the fact that sometimes we are going to write stories we don't fully understand.

Maybe here, it was the perspective that I didn't like. Maybe I felt really bad for creating Nadia and then having such a bad thing happen to her and having the narrator revel in it. Although the narrator wasn't really reveling in what happened to Nadia personally; the narrator just wanted to feed on the chaos that was created. I don't think the narrator cared about individual humans.

Back to comfort zones and non-comfort zones. Some writers don't feel comfortable writing stories of a certain length. I don't share that. Some writers really don't like writing in certain genres. I get that. Writing a Western doesn't mean simply setting your story in the West. There are many things that go into a successful story in that genre. Same with romance, same with space opera, same with every genre. It takes a lot of reading and a lot of practice and a lot of failing before we succeed. That's not necessarily a comfort zone thing, more of an experience thing. Writing in some genres is fun, and writing in some genres is not fun.

Some writers aren't comfortable writing anything explicit—for example, sex or violence. Those I get—they're difficult to write well and believably even for those experienced in writing them. Writing a main character of a different gender or race, or from an ableist point of view, those can be uncomfortable or difficult with a lack of experience. There are "sensitivity" readers and editors who can help to make that writing feel authentic.

Most of the above is for when we are writing something that will eventually go public. If you are writing something that is just for you and will only be for you, I think the rules should be different. Just write. Write whatever you like. You don't need a sensitivity editor if it's only for yourself. You don't need to learn all of the conventions of the Western genre if you are writing a Western short story just for you. If you eventually want to turn it into something for distribution or even to share with your critique group, then think carefully before sharing it. And study up on that genre and what readers of that genre expect.

But I see no reason to pull in outside folks for any reason if you are writing for yourself, especially when you are writing to push yourself into uncomfortable places. Just write, even if it's uncomfortable. Often, it's great to write when you are uncomfortable. You can't break new ground as a writer if you never leave the safety of your backyard.

Lesson learned: get out of your comfort zone and write what you normally do not like to write to push yourself as a storyteller.

HOLD MY HAND

"This is one impressive lobby."

"This is Le Domaine, Sam. One of the oldest and swankiest hotels in France. They don't call it a lobby. They call it a *fwah-yay*."

"Sometimes a lobby is just a lobby, Alex."

"Foyer, lobby, tomato, tomahto. Let's call the whole thing off."

"Clever."

"I'm serious. Let's call it off. The rehearsal dinner? The wedding? It's too much. I can't marry you."

"You've just got pre-wedding jitters, Alex."

"It's more than that, Sam. It feels wrong."

"This lobby certainly feels wrong, that's for sure. Marble floor, antique chairs, all that gilding. This isn't us. But it's what you wanted. What your family wanted, anyway."

"Every to-be-wed Compton jets across the Atlantic to get married right here, in this venerable hotel. It's our family tradition—and so are broken marriages. Sam, it's not this place that's making me question things. Okay, not *just* this place. It's everything. I'm sorry. I'm a mess."

"So let's sit on one of these historic couches for a minute. Talk to me, Alex."

"Oh, Sam. I've loved you since day one. But I've been thinking."

"You mean overthinking."

"Shut it. We don't have enough in common. I'm big city. You're small town. We Comptons are diplomats, and we're always in the press. You have no family, and you shun the spotlight. I'm young. You're—"

"Watch it."

"—not quite as young as me. And you've been married before. You've seen how a marriage can dissolve. I couldn't take it if that happens to us."

"Who thinks that's going to happen to us?"

"Who thought it was going to happen in your first marriage? We don't even understand each other's jobs. You don't know anything about diplomacy, and I don't know anything about magic tricks. We don't have enough in common, Sam. We're too different. It'll never work."

"So, you want someone more like you. Someone with cold feet, apparently. Let me ask you this: would you marry you?"

"God, no. I could never be with someone as neurotic as me."

"Well, I can. I'm telling you, Alex, we're as perfect for each other now as the day we met. And I'm going to prove it to you. With this."

"You brought a deck of cards to our rehearsal dinner?"

"You know that I never go anywhere without a deck. Besides, these cards will prove that we're perfect together."

"I smell a ruse. But I do love watching you shuffle."

"Flattery will get you everywhere. Here's how this works. I'm going to tell you three things that I want in a partner. After I say each thing, you pick a card, and that card will back up what I say."

"Like a tarot reading?"

"Pretty much. Each card in a standard deck of 52 has a deeper meaning. So let's see what the universe wants to tell us. Ready?"

"This sounds stupid. But yes, I'm ready."

"First, I believe that opposites attract, but I also believe that there must be some commonality. We have so much in common. For example, we both take our jobs seriously. For me, it's performing magic tricks, and for you, it's politics. You work hard. So do I. And, like me, you don't shy away from responsibility. Now take any card."

"I'll take one from the middle. Let's see. The four of clubs."

"Clubs represent the spiritual. The four of clubs symbolizes stability and commitment—the calm during the storm. That describes both of us, Alex. We are stronger together than when we are apart."

"That was just luck. But this is charming, Sam. Keep going."

"Second, I believe that being a couple shouldn't define us. We can't lose our own identities. I need the best parts of me, the strongest parts, to flourish. You need the same. There are three parts to our marriage: you, me, and us. You have always let me be me, and I promise I'll always let you be you. Take another card."

"The nine of hearts."

"Hearts signify emotions, feelings, and love. The nine of hearts represents contentment—knowing that being alone does not equal loneliness. We are content when we are together. See? The universe is guiding you."

"How do you know this stuff?"

"As you should know by now, I have many talents."

"Don't make me blush."

"Speaking of which, the third thing. I believe that a marriage must involve physical attraction. After commitments and jobs, after everything practical, there must be something primal in a marriage. You make my knees quake and my heart race. Take another card."

"Another heart. The jack."

"The jack of hearts loves being in love. It signifies the giddiness and intensity of new love."

"That's bad, right? A marriage is new only at the beginning. Attraction and intensity fade."

"True. But the best marriages feel new every day. That's what the universe is telling us."

"This is amazing, Sam. I had no idea that you could do this."

"The readings?"

"No, making me draw the exact card that you wanted me to take. How much of this reading is true, and how much did you make up?"

"The readings for each card are real. As far as what cards you chose—well, I *am* a magician, Alex."

"No matter. It worked. I love that you did this for me. Come on. We're late to our own rehearsal dinner. We don't want to leave a roomful of Comptons waiting. Chaos will ensue. And Sam?"

"Yes, Alex?"

"Put the deck away and hold my hand while we walk."

"I always have your hand. And I'll never let it go."

FIND YOUR RHYTHM

Look past the conceits that I like to throw into short stories—here, it's all dialogue, and no clue if Alex and Sam are men or women—and this story is about rhythm. Once I found Alex and Sam's voices, I could have written those two for a hundred pages. I had found their voices and my writing rhythm.

I work with a lot of authors who are prepping their early novels for the world, through indie publishing or to get in front agents for possible representation to publishers. Most of their books won't become great novels not because of plot or character, but because the writer hasn't found and mastered their style, their rhythm. Editing can help. Coaching can help. Reading definitely helps. Massive amount of writing really helps. But not finding their writing rhythm, their confidence, is a dealbreaker.

Rhythm is hard to define for each author. Technically, it's about mastering stressed and unstressed syllables, punctuation, long and short sentences, flow. Those are the "definitions" you'll see if you look up rhythm and writing.

But it's more than that. Someone writing gorgeous literary fiction will have a rhythm that's far different than someone mastering snappy crime fiction. Each author knows just how much tension, humor, crackle, horror, and warmth they need to put into each sentence at just the right place in their book. Experienced authors have deleted far more bad sentences than most writers will ever type.

These experienced authors have developed: rhythm. Their books aren't as much a collection of strict rules as they are three hundred pages of jazz improv. When I'm editing a book, I can feel that rhythm when it's there, and I point it out and help my authors lean into it if they can't see it. Sometimes I call it their "bold" writing, the writing when they're not overthinking or worrying about all the conflicting feedback they've been told over the years, the writing where they just *feel* the words and write. I can spot it, although I usually can't define *why* I can feel it. It's just…there. When I ask my clients about certain pages that I think are bold, usually they'll say, oh, that was easy to write for some reason. They won't always be able to say why it was easy either, but it just was.

They had found their rhythm.

When authors submit sample pages to agents, rejections often say that the agent couldn't "connect" with the story. These sample pages come from the opening to the book, and authors edit the heck out of these opening pages, so those pages can feel unnatural after a while. Opening pages are tough for dozens of reasons, but when I look at opening pages, I often see a lack of rhythm, a tightness, a conservativeness to the writing, a spinning of all the wheels, a holding back. Those opening pages don't feel like the rest of the book. They're *too* polished. Often, they are trying to do way too many things at the same time. Whatever boldness was there when they were first created has long been painted over.

In "Hold My Hand," I "knew" who Alex and Sam were right away. Because the narrator would only be recording the dialogue, I got out of the two characters' ways and let them talk. They set the scene a bit for the reader, then they talked about what they needed to talk about—cold feet and marriage while they sat in a cold, stark hotel lobby and a bunch of rich Comptons waited upstairs. The writing came easily because I had developed my rhythm for Alex and Sam quickly—and I had written and discarded enough lousy stories over the years to know that when I hit my rhythm right away, I knew how to keep it going.

Now, if you ask me to define what my rhythm is for this story, I couldn't. I just know it's there. I know what Alex and

Sam would say and would not say, and how their speech patterns differed. If someone edited a line or two of dialogue and gave the story back to me, I think I'd know right away, not because it wasn't what I typed originally, but because the rhythm would be off. I'd *feel* it.

As writers, we hope that we can create a decent plot, engaging characters, key settings, and a solid structure to build the story around. We hope that whatever genre we are writing in, that we are giving readers what they expect and want. But that's more what we want as creators. As writers, we want to find our rhythm sooner rather than later. When we say things like "we want the words to flow" and "the words poured out of me," it's not just that we are fast typists—it's that we found the natural rhythm of the story.

I look back at "Chaos," the previous story. I hadn't re-read that story in a long time before building out this book. I think I had found a decent rhythm for that story. I don't like the rhythm, but it was pretty consistent, just not a natural one for me, so even reading it back, I saw that there was a rhythm, just one that fought me the whole time.

Other stories had different rhythms. The newspaper one, "One House, Two Stories," has an easy rhythm for me because I dusted off my newspaper column style. Many of the other stories have basically the same rhythm—"Avenging Annie" and "Dragon's Lair" and "Ride Captain Ride" and "Nailed It" are clearly written by the same person and have the same rhythm. "Hold My Hand" has a different rhythm, a different jazz improv feel, one that's best played in dialogue.

Rhythm is subjective, despite there being a technical underpinning to it. If you're a writer, the best way to develop it is to write a lot and then workshop your pieces in a critique group or with another writer as often as you can. Note how you felt writing each piece that you submit—did it come easily? was it a challenge? did parts feel like your "bold" writing? Then see if any of the feedback lines up with how you felt. Don't get hung up on, or overly excited by, one instance of matching or non-matching feedback—you need several rounds of feedback to start seeing patterns.

Eventually, you will start to see patterns. You'll start to "feel" your writing differently. Read it aloud to yourself, or have someone read it aloud to you, or have one of your smart devices read it to you. Then repeat that with other pieces. What you'll consider your good writing will feel differently from your writing that needs work or was a chore to write. You'll find your rhythm.

Lesson learned: when you find your writing rhythm, then write, write, write.

THEY MAKE A PRETTY GOOD SANDWICH AT PORTLY'S

At a table for two in the food court at Stonedale Mall, an average man wearing a purple tie pretends to dig into a sandwich from Portly's Subs while he scans the lunchtime crowd.

A fat man who smells like garlic drops a phone on the sandwich man's table as he walks past. The sandwich man looks at the phone, then turns and says, "Hey, you dropped something," but the fat man keeps walking.

The phone then rings, the tone loud and shrill, but the sandwich man doesn't answer it. A few people turn toward him, but he shrugs as if to say, "It's not my phone."

The phone stops ringing. Then large, garlicky hands press down hard on the man's shoulders from behind. "Do not turn around," says a voice like someone dragging a rake through wet cement. "Do not look at me. Answer the phone when it rings again." The garlicky man squeezes the sandwich man's shoulders hard, then leaves.

The phone rings thirty seconds later. The sandwich man answers. "Hello?"

"Thompson Hanson, we have your wife. We want fifty thousand dollars in the next two hours, or we will kill her." The voice is confident and strong, a man's voice with a slight nasal tone.

"I'm not Thompson Hanson," the sandwich man says. "And I'm not married. Not any longer. I don't know what you're talking about. You have the wrong guy." The sandwich man ends the call and tosses the phone on the table.

The phone rings again. The sandwich man picks it up and answers. The voice on the phone sounds more insistent this time. "Don't toy with me, Hanson. Fifty thousand dollars, or we kill your wife."

"Look, I'm not this Hanson guy."

"Of course you're Hanson. You're wearing a purple tie, and you're eating in the food court. We followed you there."

"I'm not this Hanson guy. I'll prove it. I'll take a picture of myself on this phone and send it to you. I won't look at the number. I won't write it down. I don't want to be involved." The sandwich man's voice is jittery and a little slow, as if he's stretching for some of the bigger words.

"Fine. Take a picture of yourself and send it."

The sandwich man fumbles with the phone until he figures out how to use the camera without disconnecting the call, then takes a picture of himself. He usually avoids having his picture taken, but the image is a fairly good representation of how he looks today: puffy cheeks, scraggly black hair, and eyeglasses that went out of style in the Eighties and aren't coming back any time soon. He sends the picture.

After a few moments, the voice on the phone says, "Huh. I can see why my man got confused. We were told that Hanson is wearing a purple tie and sitting in the food court. You're wearing a purple tie and sitting in the food court. But you don't look like how Thompson Hanson was described to me. Hold on." There's silence for a minute or so, then, "I'm holding a picture of Hanson. On his wedding day. You don't look like him."

"A lot of people wear purple ties."

"That's the thing. Hardly anyone wears ties. Especially purple ties. The world has changed. Quite the coincidence." The man on the phone sighs, mutters something unintelligible, then adds, "If you're not Hanson, then I need to start all over again. My man needs to buy another phone."

"He can have this one back. I won't say anything to anyone, I promise. Like I said, I don't want to get involved."

"You've said that twice, but now you *are* involved. Shoot. I can't use that phone again. I've already called it too many times as it is. What's your name, mystery man?"

"Aaron. I'm no one. I just came here for a sandwich."

The man on the phone laughs. "My man has been watching you. He says you got the sandwich at Portly's."

"Yes."

"They make a pretty good sandwich at Portly's."

"Yes, they do. So what do we do now?"

"I'll tell my man to buy another phone. You stay on the phone with me while we wait. Keep talking so I can hear if you're doing something stupid, like talking to a security guard or calling the cops. I'll tell you when he's back in the food court. Then you leave the phone on the table so we can get rid of it, then you leave the mall, then you never talk about this. Hold on."

The man on the phone comes back on the line thirty seconds later. He sounds frustrated. "My man's all set. He's out buying another phone. But where is Thompson Hanson? The wife must know. Maybe I should beat the information out of her."

"Wait. Don't do that," Aaron says quickly. "Please. I don't want anyone to get hurt."

"You won't be the one getting hurt, Aaron. What does it matter to you? You don't know her." Now the man on the phone sounds distracted. "What is taking him so long? How hard can it be to buy a phone?"

"Please," Aaron repeats. "Don't hurt the woman. I could pay you. Pay you to not hurt her."

"Why would you do that, Aaron? You don't want to be involved, remember?"

"I don't want anyone to get hurt, is all." Aaron's voice is now more jittery.

"Do you have fifty thousand dollars?"

"Wow. No. I have maybe four thousand. The rest is gone. Divorce."

"That's a shame, Aaron. A real shame. Husbands and wives should find ways to stick together. Well, I better find Thompson Hanson. I'm not prepared to stay here all day. I hadn't planned on leaving with the wife, and I can't really kidnap her in her own house. I don't know what to do." The man on the phone pauses, then continues. "I could call the husband's real cell phone. I can get that number. But he'd trace it. They can trace anything these days, right, Aaron?"

"I suppose so. I don't know how any of that works." Aaron hungrily eyes his sandwich. He pulls out his own phone, which shows no calls or texts, then pockets it and turns it off. "I have an idea. If you think that this Hanson guy is really at the mall, I could walk around and see if I can find him. Look for a guy in a purple tie. I could say he dropped the phone, give it to him, then leave. I swear that I won't tell anyone."

"Not a bad idea, Aaron. But then you'll be a suspect. Hanson is a smart guy. He's rich. He's well connected. He'll call the cops, then this will all go to pieces more than it has already.

There are cameras all over the mall. You'll never make it out of there. Then they'll use you to find me."

"I suppose you're right. I'm really out of my element here."

"Let me see if my man bought the new phone yet. I'm texting him." The man on the phone is quiet for a bit, then returns. "He says he's in line. You can buy a phone anywhere. Did he go to the busiest store in the mall? Just buy a cheap phone at the drugstore with cash, I told him."

"What did this Hanson guy do, anyway? Why are you threatening his wife and asking for money?"

"Not your business, Aaron. Not your business."

"I know. But I'm waiting here, talking, like you asked. I'm trying to pass the time. I'm really nervous. Talking calms me down."

The man on the phone chuckles. "I know that this isn't your world, Aaron the sandwich man. Let's just say that I know a guy who knows a guy who said that Hanson didn't hold up his end of a bargain, and this guy wants his money back. I don't ask beyond what I need to know, Aaron, because I'm discreet and I'm a professional."

"It sounds like you're quite the professional. I am not. You're right. This is definitely not my world."

"Be glad," the man says. "I need to speak with Hanson's wife. Hold on."

Aaron strains to hear what's happening on the other end of the phone. The food court is packed and loud. He sticks a finger in his other ear to block the chatter. He hears the man ask, "Where is your husband?"

"He's on a business trip," a woman's voice says.

"Why didn't you tell me that?"

"You never asked."

"I did ask. I asked to speak to your husband. You said you didn't know where he was."

"I didn't know where he was then, and I still don't. He told me a few hours ago that he had to take a trip. He didn't say where. So I don't know where he is, and I didn't know where he was when you asked me."

"I'm not in the mood for wordplay. Maybe I should pull out your tongue with pliers. Then we'll see how linguistic you can be." The woman screams. The man gets back on the phone. "I have to tell you, Aaron, that I'm pretty disappointed in how this day has turned out."

"Don't pull out her tongue with pliers," Aaron says, making his voice shake.

"You could hear that? Well, I'm not going to pull out her tongue. I just need her to think that." The man pauses, then adds, "It's good for her that I like scrappy blondes."

"What if I gave you my four thousand to end this? It's all I can get right now. My bank has a branch in the mall. It's all my savings and all my checking. I'm so far in debt that four thousand dollars isn't going to matter anyway."

"Why would you do that, Aaron?"

"Because I don't like it when scrappy blondes get their tongues pulled out with pliers."

"I told you, I'm not going to do that. And I couldn't take your money. It wouldn't be right. This Hanson guy can afford fifty thousand dollars and not even miss it. You can't afford four thousand. You and me, we're the same, Aaron. Just trying to do our jobs and get through the day. And this day is not going well. The wife has seen too much of me, and she's not going to say anything useful. I don't want to hurt her. But if I don't find Hanson and get that money, then that might have to change."

"Maybe I can convince her to not say anything. I could tell her to stay quiet, just like I will."

"You want to be her white knight?"

"No, I want to throw up. I just want this to stop. I just wanted to eat a sandwich in peace."

"Okay, Aaron. How about this. I need to call my man and see what's holding him up. You talk to her and try to lay some sense into her. This is ridiculous. How long does it take for one man to buy a phone"?

Aaron stands up to stretch his legs. As soon as he takes two steps away from the table, a mall sparrow swoops down and starts pecking at his Portly's sandwich.

Aaron sighs, then hears some shuffling and bumping on the line.

"You're on speaker, Aaron, so don't try anything funny. I'll be listening."

A woman's voice, frightened and tinny, says, "Hello?"

"Hello. My name is Aaron. You don't know me. What's your name?"

The woman sniffles. "Leeza."

"Leeza, the man you're with says that he wants money from your husband."

"I don't know what he's talking about. There's no cash like that here. Please. I don't want to get hurt. I don't know what's going on. Do you?"

Aaron ignores the question. "Is there something that you can give to this man to appease him? Something valuable, like art?"

"We do have some art. But I have jewelry. The jewelry is more valuable than the art, isn't it?"

"Stick to the art. Tell him that you have some very valuable art. Tell him that now."

Leeza says loudly, "We have some very valuable art. Please, don't hurt me. I'll make it worth your while."

Aaron hears the man say, "I don't know anything about art. Art is no good to me."

"Please," Leeza says, "take the art. I'll show you. You'll see. It'll be worth it."

"I'm not untying you," the man says to Leeza. "You're staying right there."

"Then look for yourself. The good pieces are in the next room. In the library."

The man says something that Aaron can't make out, then Leeza says, "No, the other room. Through the arched doorway."

The phone is silent for a few beats, then Leeza whispers, "He's in the library."

"Lean close to the phone." Thompson Hanson takes off his wig and glasses and digs out his silicon cheek implants. He whispers, "There's a hollow in the back of the pedestal holding the Van Gelder bust. There's a loaded gun and a knife in the hollow."

"So this is Tucson all over again," Leeza whispers. "You were right. They were going to find us."

"This is exactly like Tucson. You know what to do." Thompson sees the garlicky man holding a bag and walking into the food court. "I'll be home soon. There's something I need to take care of first."

USE FAMILIAR (BUT NOT PREDICTABLE) SETTINGS

There is nothing remarkable about this story—it's a typical me story in that there is some kind of con happening, the story is relatively short, nothing of great importance takes place, and it happens over about ten minutes. I included the story because I really like the setting—a mall food court.

We've all been in a mall food court, so it's easy for the reader to fill in the details we don't have to include. Readers can picture how the tables are arranged, they can smell the smells, hear the noises—they can do a lot of the scene setting instead of me doing it.

I also wanted Thompson to have a few goals in the story. One is to keep his disguise and fake persona intact for as long as possible. Another is to keep the conversation going with the man on the phone and subtly being proactive while seeming to be only reactive. Another is to find a way to talk to Leeza. And another is to really want to eat that sandwich, only to have the mall bird ruin his meal.

When I thought up this story, I didn't know anything about Thompson and Leeza except for that they were in danger and that something like this had happened before. I was rooting for them to succeed, although maybe they were the baddies. I wanted there to be some danger, although minimal, and I had no interest in extending the story beyond the end point. I had the idea for Leeza to be only a phone call away and for Thompson to be in disguise.

I needed a setting. I could have gone with something out of a standard crime procedural—Thompson in a run-down motel while on the run, or in a car outside of a lonely diner on a rainy night. Then I thought, why not a chipper, bustling mall food court? That gave me the mall birds, the burly guy buying another phone and receiving slow service, and some more conversation around mall security, plus it gave a reason for Thompson to be in disguise and being a "normal" guy just out for a lunch (why be in disguise if you're in your own car outside a diner?). Plus it made the story a little more fun and relatable

If you have a story with two spies meeting up for a handoff, maybe they meet up in a yarn shop because one of them really likes yarn and wants to buy some. Or a couple is about to have "the talk" and break up but instead of all the stereotypical places they might have it, maybe it's inside a T.J. Maxx. Nail salons, grocery stores, a Home Depot, a fast-food place at a rest area—these are all familiar settings to your readers. If you are planning to set your story in an expected setting, think about using an unexpected setting with the same plot. Can it work?

You can extend this idea to characters. If you like action movies or procedurals, you've probably seen plenty where the main character graduated "top of her class." It can get to the point where every character graduated "top of their class." Sometimes they'll add a character who was nearly thrown out in a scandal but was kept on in a technicality. It would be fun to have an FBI agent, for example, be a middling FBI agent from the start—he's okay, he graduated like in the top two-thirds of his class, but he's nothing special. He's envious of his classmates who seem to have all these special skills, but honestly, he's got none.

That's the parallel to our "familiar but not predictable" setting—most of us did not graduate at the top of our class, and when we read a new FBI book, we expect that the new hotshot agent is going to be introduced as either the "top of the class" agent or the "almost disgraced" agent. I'm rooting for Joe and Jane Normal Agent to make it into the book. And for their first case to be in a mall food court.

Lesson learned: interesting story settings are all around you—don't stick to the first setting that comes to mind.

IN THE SHOWER

I can't *wait* to smoke that—

Can I *really* shower and be on the road in ten—

"Shane, do you *have* to flush the toilet while I'm in the—"

Can't I get any privacy, for fuck's—

Why did I marry someone who's so—

Shouldn't I feel guilty hiding my smoking from him? Why don't I feel guilty? I'm an *adult,* that's why! It's one cigarette a week! It's the only thing that I look forward—

What kind of life is it when going to work early one day a week so that I can smoke a lousy cigarette is the *best* part of my week? It's because I don't *feel* any more. When did I stop—

Fifteen years old and I snuck one out of Aunt Patty's pack. I hid it under the bed for weeks! It tasted awful! But that first hit of nicotine, I can *still* feel it, it was orgasmic, it was—

I love that word! Orgasmic. I made up that word! Is orgasmic a real—

Was that first cigarette a week *after* I made out with James at Maggie's house? Or a week *before*? Definitely before! I was feeling so grown up because I had smoked my first—

James kept pushing his hand up my shirt, and I kept pushing it—

What if I had let him? Would he *still* have broken up with me when I wouldn't—

James has really let himself go. Terrible Facebook photos! I never thought he'd look so—

What do you call it when people aren't old but just look beaten down by—

Are Facebook friends *really* friends? James *was* my friend. But now he's only a Facebook friend. Friends. That word has so many meanings now! Are any of my Facebook friends *really* my—

Damn Elise Waters bitching on Facebook about the new school! There were a hundred comments! I wanted to comment, but I couldn't think of anything snarky. I never comment unless it's—

People are so riled up about the new school! I'm against it! We don't need a new school! They're always shafting those of us who can't—

I mean don't—don't have any—

If that school gets built, the taxes are going to be sky high. *Another* week's pay down the—

How many people have commented since last night? How could I not think of something snarky? Maybe something about Elise. Bitchy Elise Waters under the bridge! No, that doesn't even make any—

Did Shane really pay the credit card bill? He said he did, but that's what he had said last month, and we got a late fee. He *said* he called to get it waived. I doubt it! He never shows me the bill! One of the many things he "takes care of," meaning he doesn't want me to—

What else is he keeping from me? What could be on that bill that's so—

Still need to buy Mom's gift. Seems stupid to get someone a present just because they give birth to you and then never support your life decisions. Or aren't there when you really need—

I loved Memphis. It was so laid back. And it doesn't snow there! Does it snow there? The South has floods all the time. Are floods better than snow? They have snakes! Are snakes better than snow? How do you decide if snakes are better than—

God, Shane was so uptight at that bar. The two of us in Memphis, our "vacation," and he has to trot out his goddamned disappointed face when I bummed a—

How many times have I tried to have a little fun and he ruins—

Am I normal? I'm not normal! The only thing I feel guilty about is *smoking*? Out of everything I *could* feel guilty about, it's only about—

Almost getting caught feels thrilling. So that's two thrilling things. Smoking one cigarette a week, and almost getting caught. Double orgasmic! Is this what living dangerously feels like? Everyone used to smoke, and no one cared. It was an easier time back then! Now you're a rebel if you throw something away instead of recycling it. Now you're scorned if you smoke. Now people feel sorry for you if you can't have—

When did I become a person who hides the best parts of myself? That's not how I want to—

I don't give a shit what *work* people think of me. I don't give a shit what my *mother* thinks of me. I don't give a shit what *Shane* thinks of me. How can I be a rebel if I give a shit what other—

Why can't I live the life I *want* to live? Why can't I just be *me*? Are they going to carve on my tombstone, "She made everyone but herself happy"? Do I really need acceptance that—

Having secrets *is* pretty thrilling. Everyone hates smoking, that's why I keep it a secret, but I must have plenty of other—

People in Memphis don't care who smokes! It's a different culture there. A Southern culture! It's definitely an easier way to live. Live and let live. Just like McCartney sang! Wait, that's live and let—

Pretend we move to Memphis. Who am I kidding? Shane isn't going anywhere! He'd never leave—

Pretend *I* move to Memphis. I can be a different me. My *true* me. The me I'm *meant* to be. A true Memphisian! Memphisonian? Memphisite? What do they call—

You know how you meet someone and they don't know anything about you and they think that their *first* impression of you is who you *really* are? Say the first time someone meets you, you're smoking. They could know you for forty years, you could end up being their best friend, and they'd think you're a smoker, even if the *first* time they saw you smoke was the *last* time you ever smoked. Isn't that funny? I think that's so—

Every person I've ever met who's been drunk when I met them, I always think of them as drunk, because of that first time. That's who they are to me. Permanently drunk! And every time I meet someone who's laughing, I think they're always happy, because they were—

Doesn't everyone think like that? They must! Everyone thinks the same way, because we're all human! But how differently do I think than everyone—

Does everyone see the same colors? Like is my blue someone else's—

Did he really just—

"Did you just flush the toilet *again*? I'm *burning up* in here! Thanks a *lot,* Shane!"

I can't—

How do you set up a new life? How much money could I get today? All of it? How long until he'd notice? A week? A day? Could I take all of our—

Where would I keep it? Definitely in a suitcase. Not in a suitcase. That's the first place they'd—

Who are *they*? Why do we always call them—

Everyone talks about going off the grid, but no one does it. Eventually you'd want Netflix because it's 2025 and that's how people live. I have no intentions of living in a crappy cabin without Netflix in the middle of—

Do I know anyone in Memphis? Maybe. I could check—

I hate Facebook! That's the first thing I'm doing when I move! Quitting is easy! I can't wait to quit—

That damn school! We don't need a new—

What if I left in the middle of the night? Or while he was at work? How long does it take to drive to—

Would he look for me in Memphis? Say he got home from work and I was gone. No note. A note that says I'm leaving, don't look for me, goodbye. Would he even look for me at all? Or would he be happy that I left? Would he even—

What the hell is *wrong* with me? I should feel—

I could leave false clues to other places in the note. Then he'd never find me! Tricky! Red clues! Isn't that what they're called? No. Red what? Red mackerel? What's the right fish? Red—

Not having kids makes traveling so much easier. We're so lucky that we don't have kids! We have so much fun *because* we don't have kids. It's just us! That's why it's fun! Most of the time it's fun. It used to be fun. But not when he gets that disappointed—

We *both* decided it was okay to not have kids. We *agreed*. Like business partners. My god. Who wants their marriage to feel like a—

We haven't talked about it in a *year*. We don't talk about *anything*. Do I even *want* to talk about—

Imaginary perfect storm. I move to Memphis. I have money. But not in a suitcase. I meet the perfect—

What if *that* guy wants kids? Why run away to Memphis to meet a guy who wants kids? That's not freedom! That's like escaping one prison and running straight into another—

How does anyone meet anyone? Dating sites? Friends? I wouldn't have any friends. I'd lose all my friends when I ran away! Maybe not *all* my friends. Some of my real friends are also Facebook friends. But Facebook friends aren't really my—

I *really* can't wait to quit—

Imaginary perfect storm. I move to Memphis. I have money. I'm hanging out downtown. I have no friends. It's sunny and warm, but I'm wearing a leather jacket! A rebel! I bum a cigarette outside of a bar and start talking to—

Could I be someone who picks up guys in a bar? Not in *this* life. A marriage shouldn't feel like a business! It should feel—

Picking someone up at a bar would be another thrill. Add it to the list! Another orgasmic thrill! That would make a good band name! Ladies and gentlemen, please welcome to the stage—

The guy outside the bar would say to his friend, did you see that woman outside the bar, the one with the long hair and leather jacket, she bummed a cigarette from me, she was hot, I'm going back out there! The guy would *totally* say that to his—

Damn Elise Waters! The last thing this town needs is a new school! Why should I have to pay for a new school when I'll never have—

"Fine, I'm done! I'm getting—"
Crap, is it already time to—
I can't *wait* to smoke that—

GET CLOSE

As I talked about earlier, there are two main points of view (POV) in fiction—first person ("I") and third person ("she"). In each, you can dive into your point of view character's head and into their thoughts as closely as you need to.

This is an extreme example of first person POV in that except for a few sentences of dialogue where the characters yells something at her husband from the shower, the story is all inner thought. I did this on purpose, from a challenge I gave myself: can I write a short story that's all fragmented, first-person inner thought?

I wanted to get as close to the character's real-time thinking as I could. This is the way that I think when I'm in the shower. I honestly thought that this is the way that *everyone* thinks. I was wrong.

I ran this through my critique groups. Some folks said that this person needs therapy, and quickly—those folks do not think like I think. Others could kind of relate. Two friends not in the critique groups said this is *exactly* how they think and it was like I was reading their minds (talking to you, Jennifer and Keely!).

Apparently, when some people are in the shower, they just shower and think standard linear thoughts? Huh!

I have no idea what "normal" means when it comes to thinking. I know that this is how I think at times, down to the cutting off of my own every thought before starting a new one and making random connections that make sense only to me. What I hoped to do here is weave this woman's connections into a story so that by the end, we can understand why she's upset at the school funding, why she's upset at her husband, and why she's holding on to this one cigarette a week—she's mourning the loss of what she can't have without directly addressing it. She's dreaming of escape and may have the same "in the shower" thoughts every day—but dreaming of change and making change are two very different things.

I could have told this story different ways and through different points of view. In normal first-person "I" stories, we could have listened in to a monologue of her thoughts:

I wish that Shane would loosen up. This one time, we took a trip to Memphis. We were both looking forward to it, maybe me more than him, but once we got there, I don't know, he was so uptight! At first, I couldn't figure out why, but eventually...

But that seems more like a long diary entry. Easy to write, but maybe not a story.

I could have turned to third person (in which case, let's call her Kendra):

Kendra lathered while wishing that Shane would loosen up. There was that time they'd taking that trip to Memphis. They'd both looked forward to it, maybe Kendra more than Shane, but once they got there, Shane had started getting uptight. It had pissed Kendra off, but she'd held it all in, or at least she'd thought she had. She...

That feels distant, more so than the first example. And if I were writing in third person, I'd have a tough time figuring out a really good way to end this. I'd have probably scrapped the story. So what if she's unhappy? It's not like anything really bad has happened to her. To me, there's less of a story here than in the first example.

But in my first person version, eavesdropping on just her inner voice for a few minutes, listening to her real-time thoughts bounce around, we get a clearer picture of what she's really worried about, how much she buries, and what it takes for her to get through each day. And we get a very clear idea of how she thinks and what kind of person she is. All readers won't think like her, and some will be turned off by the sheer amount of chaos careening around her head, but we'll get to her know her in a way we couldn't through any other point of view.

Point of view comes up a lot in my notes. Since this is first person, let's talk more about how to handle that POV.

One first-person POV advantage for writers is that when your character is thinking something, you don't always have to write, "I thought." If they see something, you don't always have to write, "I saw." Which is good, because if you had to add that every time your character saw something or thought something, the prose would get really boring! Instead, you can do something like this.

James started backing into the one empty space across the street. Parallel parking was not his jam, so I waited for the show, and I was not disappointed. A little crunch from his back bumper hitting the Toyota in back of him. A squeak as his left rear tire scraped the curb. Idiot. Eleven back and forths later, he'd wedged his Acura into a space a native New Yorker would have handled in ten seconds.

In first person, *we* take the place of the character. The words tell us what to say and feel and think and hear and taste and smell. The writer, if they've done a good job with the writing part, is controlling the reader through the whole story, giving them instructions and guiding them along. Done well, it's like the reader is wearing virtual reality glasses for an entire book, except the glasses also let them think someone else's thoughts.

But done poorly, and the reader either gets too much information (sensory overload! stop gazing at the scenery! stop describing the way the food smells!) or not enough information (where am I?) or too much thinking (I can't get out of my head!) or not enough thinking (I don't even know who I am anymore!). This will waver depending on the genre and the character and what is happening in the book (there won't be a lot of time to take in the scenery or bask in the smell of the food when the T. rex is chasing you), so the writing still has to be artful while doing what readers in that genre expect.

The best example I know of for first person POV is…you. Every second that you are alive, you are processing the world like a perfect first-person POV character in writing. You see, hear, taste, smell, feel, move, and think in real time. When you see something, you see it; you don't have to note that you see it. When you think a thought, you simply think it; you don't have to note that you thought it. Ideally, that's what writers want to give to our readers when we write in first person—except it's an edited version, because humans process so much information at the same time all the time that giving it all to the reader would be overwhelming. You have to choose what to show and include what makes sense for your story.

In my story, there is no sensory information except that the character feels the water temperature change twice when her husband flushes the toilet, and she hears him yell to her to get out of the shower at the end. There was no need for her to sense anything else—we needed to stay in her head the whole time. That would not work with most stories, unless the character was thinking about something coming up or reflecting about something in the past. And even for those, we'd usually have some clue as to where the character was.

So you've got a story idea, and you've got a preferred POV that you love to write. Be sure that it's the best way to write your story. How close do you need to be to your character to best tell that story? Or how far away? Can you stick to being in one character's head? Or do you need to jump into several characters' heads over the course of the story? And whatever you choose, is that going to be best for your readers?

Lesson learned: get as close to your character's thoughts as you can to tell the story you need to tell.

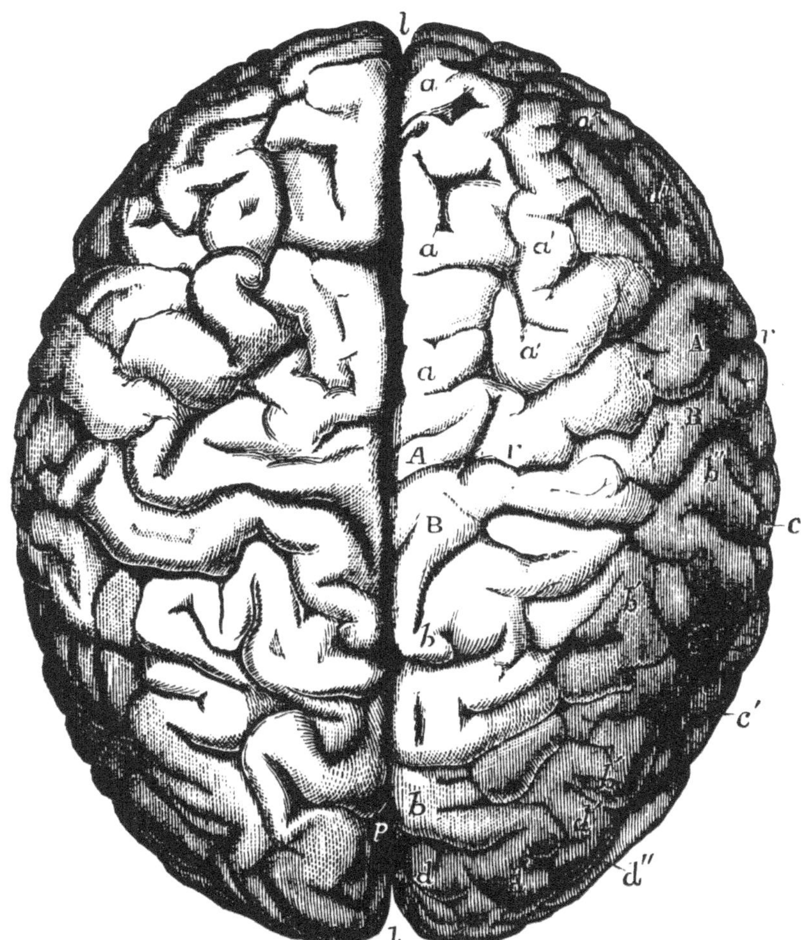

HARRY'S DINER

BUCK POND SPOTLIGHT: HARRY'S DINER
by Delia Chavez, Correspondent

Harry's Diner has been a Buck Pond tradition since 1956. For nearly seventy years, teens have giggled in the booths, children have doodled on the placemats, and couples have had first-date dinners here that led to marriages.

Although we lost Harry Turco to cancer back in 1978, his spirit lives on in his namesake eatery. We visited Harry's Diner on a picture-perfect Tuesday morning last week to witness how this local landmark continues to delight townsfolk.

Ask any local, and they'll tell you that Harry's is Buck Pond's home away from home. You can even bring your own glasses and mugs.

"I do that because the soda glasses here are too small," says Curtis Ball, who's been coming to Harry's since he was a tyke growing up on Post Hill Road around the corner. "Best to bring my own if I want a decent-sized Coke. I've seen bigger shot glasses. Harry's still a cheap bastard, even though he's long dead."

Dot Callaway, who's been slinging hash here since 1989, chuckles. "We always give Curtis an extra pickle with his ham salad sandwich to staunch his complaining," she says. "He's a peckerhead. A peckerhead who doesn't tip, I might add." A bundle of energy who never stops moving, Dot greets both regulars and first timers with her trademark, "Grab any seat, honey!"

"Speaking of grab any seat, Dot had a great ass back in her day," Curtis says. "You could bounce a quarter off her rump, and it wouldn't hit the floor for five minutes."

Phil McLeish, who grew up next door to Curtis and is seated across from him in a classic red vinyl booth so evocative of the diner age, agrees. "Dot lives on my street, and late at night I sometimes hunch down real close to the hedges around her house and peek through her windows. Been doing it for twenty years. She never sees me. I could almost reach out and grab her." He holds out his index finger and thumb. "I've this close so many times."

"Phil used to slap my ass in here all the time," Dot says. "Hard, too, and in a mean way. He still would if he weren't so arthritic. He's an awful man. He stopped after I told him that I was going to cut off his arm with a cleaver and jam the bloody limb down his throat until he choked to death. Meant it, too."

Folks love Harry's for the atmosphere, but you can't beat the food. For starters, there's always a soup of the day, advertised as homemade but most often poured from cans that sat in a warehouse for months before the distributor got around to filling the order. Sometimes the cans are bulging.

"You never tasted clam chowder until you've tasted Harry's clam chowder," says Peggy Boyle. Peggy's worked the register for a dozen years, never missing a day, even during the ice storms that shut down County Road 29 and trap the Buck Pond residents in their homes with the spouses and children they hate.

"Ain't that the truth!" says Hoss Shump, who is sharing a breakfast with his wife of forty years, Ruby. Hoss and Ruby live so close to Harry's that they can walk, or they could before the county expanded the road to two lanes both ways and took out the sidewalks. It's common here to see a careless deer ripped in two by a big rig roaring through town. Ruby sometimes imagines shoving Hoss into the path of a truck just to see what would happen. She bets his body would just explode.

Desserts are a Harry's specialty. From the decadent chocolate cake with rich frosting that's brought on several widowmakers and the signature triple-layer coffee cake to the succulent apple pie and the lemon meringue with a crust so big and stiff that you'd swear you were eating the sail of a desiccated Portuguese man o' war, customers never leave Harry's hungry.

Peggy Boyle not only works the register, she keeps the dessert fridge stocked. "I don't touch the sweets, though," she says as she bustles about. "I'd weigh a thousand pounds if I ate dessert every day." Which she nearly does, and which she does. Peggy also keeps a baggie of crushed peanut powder under the register and sprinkles it on the puddings of the customers she loathes, hoping to kill someone by anaphylactic shock. She's caused thirteen episodes, but none fatal, and the last was three years ago, so she feels overdue. She thinks about killing by anaphylaxis every day. It's the only thing that gets her out of bed every morning. That, and gravity.

The dinner menu is highlighted by the pot roast, a hunk of slow-simmered beef or other available meat slathered in gravy and served with mashed potatoes and a second side of your choice. "I remember when the gravy had those little onions in it," says Maxine Knight, who's nearly 80 but looks 110. Maxine was quite the looker back in the Sixties. Now, simply putting on a shawl causes her to bruise, and when she picks at a hangnail, her fingertip bleeds. "The cook back then was a man named Jackson. He made a great sauce. He'd give you two rolls without you even asking. It was a sad day when Jackson left."

Maxine's daughter Jesse, herself a Harry's regular, smiles warmly across the table at her mom. Jesse craves the day when she gets the call that Maxine has passed. "Mom, you know they ran him out of town because he was stealing. Heck, they even burned down his house!"

"His gravy was delicious." Maxine says. She looks longingly at the hallway leading to the restrooms. "I miss smoking so much. There used to be a cigarette machine over there. You'd drop in your quarters, pull the lever, and get yourself a fresh pack of Chesterfields. Life was fun back then. Now everyone I know is either dead, waiting to die, or"—she narrows her eyes at her daughter—"waiting for *me* to die."

Jesse beams at Maxine. "You've always loved it here, Mom!"

"I got impregnated in that restroom," Maxine says. "You're not your father's child. You're Harry's girl. I never liked Harry much, but that man could screw like a banshee. My late husband, now he was a lousy lay."

It's the service that keeps people coming back to Harry's. "We sure know our customers," says Lorenzo Kane. He and his wife Camilla took over the diner last year, adding some Mexican and Asian flair to the menu. "We know that Curtis gets that extra pickle, or that Fay Johnson always takes lemon in her water. They don't have to ask for those things. You take care of your customers, and your customers will take care of you."

Lorenzo's real name is Evan Philbrick. Camilla's real name is Becky Fletcher. They've bled Harry's nearly dry, as they've done to three restaurants before this. Harry's Diner will be consumed in a fire next month. Evan and Becky have already picked out a new target in Shreveport—the insurance money from Harry's should more than cover it—as well as a new owner for the soon-to-be burned-out diner's acreage.

"It's going to be one of those medical office buildings," Lorenzo/Evan says. "The kind they can build in a week. The developer has been begging me to sell since the day I signed the papers to buy this dump. My new name will be Reggie, and Beck settled on calling herself Dover. Sounds like a stripper name, but Beck looks like a stripper, so whatever. I can't wait to leave Buck Pond. The winters are miserable, and the locals are bigots." He pauses to greet frequent customer and Buck Pond Bank & Trust manager Tom Fairley with a big smile and a friendly wave. "If someone in town had spent even ten minutes checking into my background, they'd learn that I'm not who I say I am, but even that's too much work for a bunch of racist, illiterate hicks."

"I stopped coming here when they stopped providing copies of the *Tattler*," Tom says, sliding into the booth next to Curtis and signaling to Dot for some coffee.

"Then why'd you start coming back?" Phil asks.

"Because the whole town is gentrifying before my eyes," Tom replies. He gazes out the window at the traffic creeping through Buck Pond with the rheumy eyes of a diseased bloodhound. "It's the only honest place to eat left in town. All these hippie places with their Vegemite options."

"I think you mean vegan," Curtis says. He wonders how Tom can tie his own shoes, let alone manage a bank. "And they're called hipsters now, not hippies."

"You can call them what you want. They can all go to hell," Tom mutters.

If you want to experience Buck Pond like a local, stop by

Harry's Diner. Come for the food, but stay for the local color. Like the sign out front says: "Harry's Diner, Just Like Home!"

TELL US WHAT THEY AREN'T SAYING

One of the many advantages of writing is that it's quick and efficient to "hear" a character's thoughts. If you are writing in first person, as I've talked about earlier, you don't have to add "I thought" to your sentences.

~~Jim is an idiot, I thought.~~
Jim is an idiot.

When writing in third person ("Kylie walked to the door"), you make the decision how close you get to the character's thoughts—in effect, how much of what they think the reader gets to listen into.

One way I like to think of "closeness" is using a camera as an indicator. This camera records audio and video and all the other senses—and also records character thoughts.

If you are writing about a sweeping battle scene and you want to give the reader an indication of the scope, you might position that camera above the battle so the reader sees how huge and chaotic the scene is. Here, you aren't focusing on one character, so that camera isn't listening to any one character's thoughts.

Then you swoop down to a character in the battle, Giles, who is running for his life. The camera is then perched on Giles' shoulder. The reader sees what Giles sees, hears what

Giles hears, and "hears" what Giles is thinking. That's a closer point of view.

In first person, and in really closely written third person, that camera is inside the character, basically in their brain, recording everything in real time and passing whatever the author chooses along to the reader.

So here in "Harry's Diner," I took the conceit of a newspaper article, which is written in third person, but added in what the people being interviewed, and in a few places, what Delia Chavez, the writer, were thinking, and passed those thoughts off as if they were dialogue or, in Delia's case, as commentary.

It's an extreme example of using inner thought, but one I hoped would be fun to play around with. When I used to interview people for newspaper articles, there was what they said, and there was what they didn't say, and there was *always* something they didn't say—I just never knew what that was.

Locals love their local landmarks, so articles like this story in a local newspaper are basically public relations pieces and free advertising—they're always going to be positive.

In print.

But I know that if I ask someone who's been going to the same diner, for example, for forty years to describe the place without a filter, they're going to have some bad memories mixed in with the good. Maybe some evil memories. Maybe some evil current thoughts. I'm never going to hear those. But I know that they're there.

So this piece was just a fun way of playing around with the idea of Delia having that point of view camera, asking her questions, and being able to instantly plop that camera inside her interviewee's head. She also plopped it into her own head. So we got to hear what was said, and what was not said, by anyone Delia chose, including herself.

When we write in first person, we can always catch the

difference in truth between what our character says and what our character thinks. We can do the same when we have are in the head of our third-person characters.

But what's really fun is when readers know that a character is lying, and all the other characters know that that character is lying, but no one is doing anything about it.

Sa you're a hitchhiker, soaked from the rain, and you lurch into a bar late at night. You're shaken after getting dropped off in the middle of this little town, because you've heard all the howling from the woods, and the trucker who dropped you off told you he wasn't going to take you any farther, he just couldn't, it wasn't safe for either you or him, and there's no one else on the streets, and when you entered the bar, the place fell silent. You ask if anyone else heard the howling.

"Just loons on the lake," someone murmurs, and the rest of the heads nod and say, "Just the loons."

It's already eerie, and both the hitchhiker and you the reader know that everyone is lying, but you also both know that no one is going to tell you the truth, at least not know.

Or you show up to the wake of a cousin you haven't seen for forty years, you don't really know the guy at all, and when you get there, the crowd is sparse, only five people, you can sense right away that something's off because all five people who are there speak a language your cousin never spoke, and all you get from the four of the five is the same pat answer: "he was a helluva guy, helluva guy." The fifth guy is whispering into a phone the whole time. You say you didn't know your cousin, didn't even know what he did for work. "Helluva guy," they say.

In both these cases, the mystery might be getting to the truth of what isn't be said: what is up with this small town? or what was your cousin involved in? Eventually, the story will get to what wasn't being said.

More immediately, in our writing, we can use many tricks to have characters say one thing but really mean another.

You ask how your new boss is, and you get a heavily sarcastic reply like, "Oh, she's *fantastic*."

You ask someone else what it's like to work here. Someone replies with a deadpan expression, "You'll love it."

Someone else adds, "Yeah, you'll never forget this place."

There is a form of writing called third person omniscient, where the narrator can pop into any character's head at any time, changing the point of view even line to line. It's quite a hard writing form to master; if not done well, it can really confuse readers, because they don't know who the point of view character is supposed to be.

Now if you want to write in an experimental form, which I've done here, it's easier to jump from head to head, because if you've opened the story correctly, you've already introduced the reader to your experimental structure, and if you've done it well, it's like you've made them a promise and they've accepted it. You've promised them weirdness from the start, so they'll more readily accept you jumping from head to head.

(All writing is like that, honestly—the writer starts on page one, and from the opening word, they're making the reader a promise of sorts: "Trust me, I got this. See what I've done so far? There's more of that, and it's only going to get better. You in?" That's your reader promise!)

But because you're being experimental, your reader may be more apt to be okay with you jumping from head to head without it being off-putting to readers. I see that head-hopping done a lot in client work where it's been done mistakenly—it sticks out because the writer's promise to the reader has been, say, third-person, with one POV character, then we get to a scene where we are suddenly in everyone's heads, then we are back to one POV character. Sometimes it's meant to be clever, but unless the writer is really strong, it's best to not shoot for incredibly clever—it usually does not work nearly as well as the writer thinks it does. An editor's job is to not only lift the writing, it's to take on the role of the reader advocate and make sure that the writing doesn't pull the reader out of the story.

As in life, in your fiction, there is what is on the surface, and there is what lies beneath the surface, and there is usually a LOT more beneath the surface. Readers want complex characters. I'm not saying that every character has to constantly lie. But readers want characters to have turmoil, to be under pressure, to have secrets.

Lesson learned: what your characters don't say is just as important as what they do say.

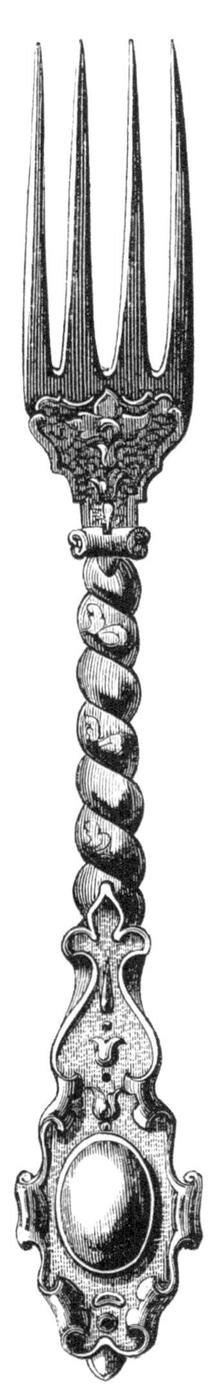

LITTLE DEVILS

"Thanks for inviting us," Tanya says to Jocelyn. The two moms are sitting on a bench at the playground. The sky is a mix of sun and volcanic plumes, the temperature a pleasant 320 degrees, and the light breeze carries the scent of decay. "This is such a pretty park."

"My pleasure," Jocelyn replies. "It must be hard, being new in town. I'm so glad that you joined us! We hold these 'Mommy and Me' playdates every Tuesday morning until school starts. Gotta keep the little demons busy!"

The kids seem like a well-behaved bunch, Tanya thinks. Three of them are screaming and kicking at each other as they build and then destroy sulfur castles in the sulfur box. Four others have stuffed a smaller kid in a duffel bag and are hitting him with lengths of pipe, while another group joins some parents in whipping rocks at nests of flame-bats.

Tanya sighs. She wishes that her son Johnny was more of a joiner and didn't misbehave so often. These kids are the sort of demons he could use for friends. They'd be good influences.

"Which one is your boy again?" Jocelyn asks Tanya.

Tanya looks around, then spots Johnny, sitting by himself on a rock in a pool of lava near where flames lick at the edge of the playground. She points. "The one with the blue jacket."

"What is that he's doing?" Jocelyn asks, her brow furrowing.

Tanya takes a deep breath before answering. "He's... doodling," she says softly.

"Oh," Jocelyn replies after a beat. "He's being so...quiet."

"They say he'll grow out of it," Tanya says quickly. "I think he's just trying to get attention. The divorce and the move have been hard on him. Which kid is yours?"

"The blonde in green," Jocelyn answers. Tanya sees a group of five kids swinging pole saws at each other and hacking off each other's limbs.

"I'll introduce you to my little hellion," Jocelyn says. "Ashley!" she screams. "Get your tail over here!"

Ashley gallops over. She is cradling her severed arm. "Look what happened to me, Mommy!" she says brightly.

"That's great!" Jocelyn says. "I'm glad you're having fun, honey."

"She looks just like you," Tanya adds, relieved to not be talking about Johnny's misbehavior. "She's got your tusks."

"That's mostly from my husband's side. He's full Nazgul. I'm only half." Jocelyn rummages through her bag as she asks Ashley, "You want a juice box?"

"Yes!" Ashley shouts, defiantly jamming her arm back onto her body and flexing her claws. "One with a straw. A big, big straw. I want to throw a billion zillion straws in the ocean!"

"Aww," Tanya says. She wishes that Johnny would talk sweet like that. "She's a precious little thing."

Ashley snaps her jaws at Tanya.

"She's very spirited," Jocelyn says as Ashley snatches the juice box from her. "Now *that* she gets that from me." Then to Ashley, she adds, "Ash, why don't you take a juice box over to

Tanya's son Johnny? He's sitting on that rock in the lava pool."

Ashley looks at Johnny, then laughs. "That kid? The one who's *drawing*? I'm not bringing him a juice box! He's *not* an acid face and he *doesn't* smell!"

"Ashley!" Jocelyn sputters. She sounds mortified, but Tanya has heard plenty of kids talk about Johnny like that before. It comes with the territory when your kid acts out in public.

Jocelyn says sternly to Ashley, "Young lady, what did you *really* mean to say?"

Ashley stomps her cloven hooves a few times, then mutters, "Fine. Johnny *is* an acid face. His face is *full* of acid. And he smells *really* bad. But I'm still not bringing him a juice box." She then runs to rejoin the pole saw kids.

"I'm sorry about that," Jocelyn says, putting the juice box away. "Kids. Honestly, I don't know where they pick that stuff up. She's never like that at home."

"It's fine," Tanya replies. "Obviously, I'm dealing with behavior issues of my own." She turns to see Johnny walking over to her. "Speaking of the little angel," she adds under her breath.

"Hi, Mom," Johnny says when he reaches the bench.

"Johnny, this is Mrs. Hunter," Tanya says.

"Hi," Johnny says, adjusting his glasses and smiling. "It's good to meet you, Mrs. Hunter."

"Wow," Jocelyn says, sounding shocked. "I mean…hello, Johnny."

Johnny turns to Tanya. "Mom, I was thinking…when I grow up, I want to help people."

Jocelyn gasps. Tanya hears one of the parents sitting behind her say a little too loudly, "He's a little *saint*, is what he is."

"Oh my gods, Johnny," Tanya says, feeling mortified. "This has to stop. Don't you want to go blow something up? Or steal a soul? Maybe take a turn hitting that kid in the duffel bag with the pipe?"

"I'm good," Johnny says. He starts walking back to the rock, adding over his shoulder, "I'm going to go draw some pictures of world peace. See you, Mom."

"We're going to talk about this later!" Tanya yells after him. When he's out of earshot, she turns to Jocelyn. "Now it's my turn to be sorry. That outburst…maybe coming here today wasn't such a good idea."

Jocelyn pats Tanya's leg with her claw. "I'm sure it'll work out," she says. "He's new in town. He's adjusting." Then she leans in and whispers conspiratorially, "Our oldest was a bit like that when she was little."

"Really? What did you do?"

"Parenting 101," Jocelyn replies. "First, we ignored her, then we deprived her of sleep and water. Eventually, things changed for the better, and she became far more destructive and self-centered. It was just a stage she was going through."

"The loving approach," Tanya says. "Got it. Guess I'll keep trying."

"Little demons need help becoming big demons."

"Amen to that."

"Ooh, I do love a mom who swears!" Jocelyn says, laughing. "Once the kids are in school," she adds, "most of us parents still get together on Tuesday mornings. Walking, coffee, some mutual beheading. Helps us to lose our sanity. Parenting is tough. It'd be great if you could join us."

Tanya brightens. "Thank you. I'd like that!"

She smiles to herself as she turns to watch the kids play. Maybe with some time and impatience—and the help of a new friend—she *and* Johnny will adjust.

WRITE PLAYFULLY

Writing toward a goal—a novel's first draft, a short story deadline—is a great motivator, especially when there is money on the line. But sometimes we need to write just for fun.

Writing for fun lets us play with language and words, experiment with different forms and genres, and most importantly, practice, practice, practice. Every time we write, we become a better writer, and if the only time we write, we're doing it while working on our Great American Novel, we're always working toward a goal and never really writing for fun and exercise.

That can mean we're never writing in a totally relaxed fashion. We're not writing "loose." We're always writing with a fear that we're making mistakes, because this writing "counts." We're never practicing.

Playful writing—writing that doesn't "count"—makes us better writers. Now by playful, I don't mean that the tone always has to be playful, like here in "Little Devils" (this is the lightest piece in this book, maybe tied with "Nailed It"). Your practice playful pieces might be serious, tearful stories full of depth and meaning. As long as they get you writing, consider them playful in the way I'm using that word here.

One thing that happens when we sit down to free write is that we can spend a long time trying to figure out what to write, then the playful part goes out the door. Writers don't like staring at a blank page even when it's just for practice. Blank pages mock us.

My way of avoiding staring at a blank page is what I did for "Little Devils"—think of an ordinary situation (here, a playdate at the park) and then make some aspect of that situation 180 degrees from normal (the parents and kids are demons instead of humans). Then it's really easy for me to start writing right away. The first draft of this story, at just over a thousand words, took probably thirty minutes of free writing, then I took a few passes at cleaning it up (because even the first draft of a short story is a messy first draft—and it should be messy!) and in a few hours, the story looked nearly identical to the version here.

Playful writing like this also helps us practice starting, revising, and finishing, and that is super important. Every story, no matter how short, has a beginning, a middle, and an end. The more stories we create, draft, revise, polish, and complete, the more times we tussle with beginnings, middles, and endings, and the more times we go from a first draft to a completed draft, and the more times we work to make a piece feel consistent. If we do that only in a book, and we plan to only write a few books in our life, then we never get the practice we need to tackle the really hard parts of writing—and those hard parts aren't typing words. Typing words is the easiest part of writing a book. The hard parts are learning to finish, learning to revise, learning to "feel" the different parts of our story. Short stories are fantastic ways to practice those parts of writing.

When we are in the middle of writing a novel, and our writing time is limited, it's easy to conclude that all of our limited writing time should be spent on the novel. But if we give ourself permission to take some time to play, to write outside the novel, to make mistakes that don't matter and create characters and scenes that have nothing to do with that novel and write for the sheer fun of writing, we'll make our novels better even with that limited writing time.

Lesson learned: give yourself more time to write for the sheer fun of it.

I WANT YOU

"Aren't you coming up to bed?" Cassie asks her husband Kevin.

"I'm going to watch the end of the game," Kevin replies, slumping on the couch. "Be up later."

"Fine." Cassie tromps away and up the stairs to their bedroom.

Kevin sighs. Fourteen years of marriage, and now he and Cassie are just going through the motions, being fake-happy in front of the kids and indifferent in front of each other. The only action that their bedroom has seen in months is arguing and the occasional vacuum.

This, he thinks, is a stupid way to live.

Kevin needs to wind down. He's just returned home from the end-of-season town youth soccer coach and volunteer appreciation banquet at the Twisted Pickle, the local dive bar. Although it wasn't really a banquet—everybody paid for their own weak beer and soggy nachos. It was just a gathering to wrap up the season. Cassie wasn't happy that he'd gone and left her with the kids, but what was he supposed to do? Besides, she was the one who suggested he volunteer to coach and get out to meet more people, even though he knew next to nothing about soccer.

Kevin snaps off the lights and snaps on the TV, muting the volume so it won't disturb Cassie and the kids. He doesn't know if there is a game on, but with all these channels, there has to be something to watch. It doesn't matter what the sport is—he'd suffer through cricket if he can have the next 30 minutes to himself and dodge another late-night discussion with Cassie about what he thinks their problems are.

His phone continues to buzz incessantly. There has been a big group text among the coaches as they'd planned the (non) banquet, and the thread is still alive with post-Pickle chatter—had a great time, so nice to see everyone, thanks for all your help, what a crazy night.

Crazy night? Kevin didn't see anything crazy. It's always the same people all the time. This is a small town, and they're all middle-aged youth soccer coaches. How much crazy can there be?

He clears the group text, and as he does so, another text arrives, this one just to him, from Jamie Winters, one of the other coaches. She'd been at the Pickle tonight. Jamie is quiet and smart, and cute in that "suburban soccer mom who goes to the gym and never stops moving" way.

Kevin flicks open the message. Jamie had written:

You could tell I wanted to say something else, but I couldn't in front of all those people. I do now. I want you.

Holy hell, Kevin thinks, stunned. Holy hell in a holy hand basket. He shuts off the television and sits in the dark and rereads the text a dozen times.

Jamie Winters?

Jamie Winters wants *him*?

Kevin puts his phone down, closes his eyes, and feels both nausea and a thrill course through his body. He's used to feeling nauseous, what with work and eating poorly and all the spousal arguing, but the thrill? He hasn't felt thrill in years.

He opens his eyes, picks up his phone, and starts to reply, but then he stops, as he has no idea what to write.

Jamie Winters wants him.

Jamie Winters wants *him*?

What had Jamie said to him? What had he said to her? What had he missed?

He pictures them talking. He'd been leaning against a wall, watching the group. He'd never been much of a joiner and had had zero interest in talking about soccer. Jamie had strolled past, then stopped and turned. They had talked for a few minutes, just non-soccer chit-chat. Jamie was always funny. Quirky. And drama-free. Kevin had never heard any gossip about her, which meant that she was either incredibly boring or incredibly discreet.

Had either of them said anything unusual? He replays the conversation as best he can. There was that one story about that rainy day, a Saturday when he and Jamie had been coaching on adjacent fields. It had started to pour, and all the kids and coaches had huddled under Kevin's pop-up tent. Jamie had asked if he remembered that day. Of course he had, he told her. He didn't add that he had liked standing next to her under his pop-up tent as the rain fell, because who doesn't want to spend a few minutes helping keep a pretty woman dry? That was the most time he had ever spent with Jamie, tonight included.

There *had* to be something he'd missed tonight.

Let's see. He had stayed in his knot for the most part, with the fourth- and fifth-grade coaches, with Sheehan and Meghan and that Paul, while Jamie had mostly stayed in her knot, the third-grade coaches plus Fitzy and short Kenny and tall Kenny.

People stuck to their knots at group things. Short Kenny coached the youngest kids. Did tall Kenny coach the sixth graders? Or was he even a coach at all? Kevin couldn't recall. Maybe tall Kenny had been in the Twisted Pickle anyway and had wandered over to their group. There weren't many other places to go in this town on a Friday night.

He pulls up Jamie's Facebook profile on his phone, but since they aren't Facebook friends, he can't see many pictures of her. Her profile picture is her with her kids, of course. He scrolls. There are a few public pictures of her. Hazel eyes, a scattering of freckles about her nose and cheeks, long brown hair in a ponytail. A genuine smile even when she takes a selfie, not that duckface thing that everyone seems to do, including Cassie. Actually, Kevin realizes, Jamie is more than pretty. Jamie is hot.

And hot Jamie Winters wants him.

But...why?

Was there a spark between them tonight? If there was, would he have even noticed a spark? They had talked about that rainy Saturday, and a few other things, and before she drifted away, she said nice talking to you, Kevin, and gave him a smile.

Was it a bigger smile than usual? He doesn't know how big she usually smiles. Did her smile linger? Maybe it wasn't what she had said—it was what she *hadn't* said. He was meant to pick up on something. He wishes she had been more obvious— he's terrible at picking up on some things. Whatever it was, it couldn't have been something overt. People would have noticed, especially in a tight room full of gossipy hens and roosters. He certainly hadn't made a move. He hadn't even thought about making a move.

He chuckles. What move? He doesn't *have* moves. He hasn't made a move in almost two decades. Jamie, however, *had* made a move. She had texted him. She isn't only hot and quirky and drama-free. She's *bold.*

Kevin takes a deep breath, exhales, then shakes his head. Spark, linger, move—this is ridiculous. He'll never know what is going on until he talks with Jamie.

So he has to text back. He has to be bold, like her.

He flicks open the message app—then puts the phone back down.

He misses being bold. Back in the day, he had been bold. He had pursued a career, had wooed women, Cassie included. Had Cassie ever been bold? All Cassie was now was unhappy. And he was unhappy. He didn't talk to Cassie about anything except work and the kids, and she didn't talk to him about anything except work and the kids. Neither of them was happy, and neither of them was bold.

Jamie Winters wants *him.*

Is she as unfulfilled in her marriage as he is in his? She has to be. Why else would she have texted him?

What is Jamie's husband's name? Matt or Mark, definitely. Liam?

Jamie Winters wants *him.*

Kevin picks up his phone, then drops it back on the couch again and puts his head in his hands.

Jamie. Winters. Wants. *Him.* And. He. Has. No. Idea. What. To. Do.

This is big, he thinks, pressing his palms against his closed eyes. This is a defining moment. This is a fork in the road of life.

Kevin gets up, gets a drink of water, then returns to the couch.

He continues thinking in the dark. What do you do when big moments arrive? Do you shy away, or do you grab them? Do you live in the past, fearful of the future, or do you live for today?

Too often, Kevin knows, he has shied away from big moments. Kids and age and a stale marriage and a career that is nothing more than a job without passion have all worn him down, made him afraid to leap. Because leaping means taking a chance, and taking a chance means potential failure, and isn't it better to stay on the safe road than to fail?

Kevin runs a hand through his thinning hair. This is a pivotal moment, he realizes. This is bold time. And if he doesn't take a chance now, if he doesn't leap, he may never get another chance, because the safe road never has forks and chances to leap come along far less often than we think when we are young.

His heart now hammering, he picks up his phone.

Another text from Jamie:

Kevin OMG 😳 please reply

His heart hammers even more. He's taken too long to text back! He squints at the screen. Which emoji is that? What does it mean? Why do they have to make them so small?

He takes a deep breath. It's now or never, and he's sick of his answer always being "never."

Kevin shakily replies:

I wanted to say the

Crap, he hit send before he finished. He starts the text again, his quaking fingers mashing out the rest of his message, but before he hit send, he gets an immediate reply from Jamie:

You can't tell anyone about this

Kevin, now grinning as his heart continued to pound, deletes what he's been typing, then replies:

I won't. I promise.

Another immediate reply from Jamie:

**Thank god you figured it out that text was a mistake
didn't mean to send it to you
I know too many Ke guys** 
please please please don't tell anyone ok?

She texts again:

**Please don't tell Elliot about Kenny
I'm not a horrible person. E and I are not in a good place. It's a
long story I can't share. Thx J**

Kevin, no longer grinning, drops his phone and thinks—about Jamie and Cassie, about being bold and staying safe, about roads taken and roads ignored. Then he picks up his phone and types out a text to his sleeping wife.

GIVE YOUR CHARACTERS FLAWS

Do you remember that time you said that stupid joke in front of that group of strangers twenty years ago? Of course you do. None of them remember it. In fact, no one else on the planet remembers it. Except you. And you'll never forget it.

Now that is good writing fodder!

Simple mistakes can kick off interesting stories. Here, Kevin isn't the one who made the mistake—it was Jamie who texted Kevin by mistake. If Kevin hadn't spent so much time in his head thinking about Jamie and had given in to his impulses right away, he would have texted her back just a minute or so earlier, and since we don't know Jamie, we don't know what she would have done with that information. That would have made a very different story, and Kevin would have made a really big mistake that he'd remember forever, although I bet he'll remember this night forever anyway.

I am one of those people who remembers a lot of the dumb things I've done, silly innocuous things that no one else remembers or even should remember. Sometimes my mouth makes decisions before my brain has a chance to weigh in, then my brain keeps an immaculate inventory of those decisions.

Maybe it's the writer in me that won't let me forget those things. But I have found that the one way I can let go of some of those "dumb but no one else remembers them" things is to use them in stories.

Our characters should be flawed, and an easy way to make them flawed is to look first at our own flaws. Those flaws don't have to be the big flaws, the stereotypical trope flaws found in so many books—the grizzled police veteran drinking to forget; the divorced dad living in a cramped, dirty apartment doing anything he can to win back the love of his kids; the middle-aged woman still living at home and taking care of her domineering mother, too beaten down to ever find happiness and love. These come up in fiction all the time, to the point where when a character is introduced as "divorced dad," we can almost smell the empty pizza boxes before we walk into his apartment.

As writers, we can do better. We can look at ourselves, to start.

Maybe our character's flaw is that they're socially awkward only when they introduce themselves to strangers and they immediately say something dumb. Maybe the flaw is that they can't for the life of them parallel park and they're always late to every dinner in the city. Maybe their unfounded childhood fear of squirrels forces them to never take the shortcut through the urban park and then one day they witness something shady going down in an alley and they're forced to go on the run.

In "I Want You," Kevin also is on the verge of making a potential mistake by potentially throwing his marriage away based on three minutes of "the grass is greener" thinking. I liked writing this from his point of view—it wouldn't have been much of a story if I had written it from Jamie's point of view, although we could have witnessed the moment she realized that she'd sent the text to the wrong person, and spent some time in her head as she made the decision to text Kenny and gotten some insight into her marriage to Elliot.

To me, it felt more fun to have Kevin fumble through his thinking over a few minutes, from not really feeling part of the group to almost being ready to run away with a woman he barely knows, all to capture some excitement that seemingly has been absent from his life for a quite a while. Like he went through an entire mid-life crisis in those three minutes and 1,500 words.

I'm not sure what he decided to text to his wife. I'm leaning toward something sweet and then he heads upstairs to Cassie. But there's a small part of me that wonders if he's now fixated on being bold and the roads ignored, and he's going to make a bad decision anyway.

If you're writing a character who seems a little flat, no matter the genre—even if they're an action hero—give them a flaw. I'm not talking about The Big Flaw, because every action hero has The Big Flaw. I'm talking about some little flaw that any character could have to make them more interesting. Look first to something embarrassing you did in your life, and make that happen to them. No matter what it is, it'll make your character more "human," and maybe it'll get that embarrassing moment out of your head.

Lesson learned: all characters need flaws, especially normal flaws, to be believable and relatable.

CHAPARRAL

-- DRAFT POWERPOINT PRESENTATION w/ SPEAKER NOTES --

```
[check: water, projector remote (need laser
pointer?)]
```

Thank you for the opportunity to speak to you today.

slide 1: TRT symbol

I have been asked by TRT to explain the issue in terms that the layperson can understand. Since I led the team that developed the curriculum that is now standard in our primary schools nationwide, I'll treat you all as second-graders for the next few minutes, even though this information will not be new to any of you. I promise that if you all pay attention, however, we'll have recess afterwards.

```
[pause for laughter]
```

s. 2: Emily Bostock (2123)

To review: time travel will be discovered on January 25, 2119 by Emily Bostock, a sanitation worker in Bozeman, Montana, on the morning of her 30th birthday.

Ms. Bostock, who will have had no formal science training and will not have attended college, awoke that morning with both the complete, fully-formed theory of time travel AND the knowledge of how to take it from theory into application.

s. 3: Emily Bostock at meeting at New Stanford University (2120)

Ms. Bostock didn't know what to do with this new-found and miraculous knowledge. She tried unsuccessfully to convince physicists across the nation, and later across the globe, without success,

s. 4: Valerio Nole

until she found the sympathetic ear of Dr. Valerio Nole at Italy's Università di Bologna in 2123. I don't think that there is a person on the planet who has not seen the video of their initial press conference, a press conference that won't occur for a hundred years.

[Possible interruptions here. Likely discussion points, which have been debated endlessly (point that out if needed). Some will say that since we know about time travel now, surely we'll know about it a hundred years hence, and there will be no need for Ms. Bostock. Others will say that

we will have forgotten about it in a hundred
years for reasons unknown, which is why we
will need to ensure that Ms. Bostock is born
and that time travel will be discovered then
for the first time. If discussion gets
heated, end debate with "Let's leave this
discussion to the theoretical physicists."]

s. 5: title Operation Chaparral

Building and testing the time travel equipment took the better
part of two decades. Then came Operation Chaparral, devised
by Ms. Bostock in 2149–120 years from now.

s. 6: Emily Bostock writing on ceramic box (2149)

Operation Chaparral is about helping mankind and saving our
planet, but it's also about proof—proof to us that time travel not
only is possible, but had been done—or had will be done. We all
know how confusing talking about time travel can be, especially
when it comes to using the correct verb form.

[pause for laughter]

On the morning that Ms. Bostock awoke in her cramped
Bozeman apartment with what is now known as the Bostock-
Nole Theory fully formed in her head, there was a box on the
floor at the foot of her bed.

s. 7: ceramic box in apartment

The box, constructed of an unknown ceramic and with no

apparent way to be opened, had these now-famous words written across its top: "I will open when it is time."

s. 8: ceramic box (top w/ words)

The box opened at the moment that Ms. Bostock returned to her apartment in Bozeman in 2123 after convincing Dr. Nole that her theory was real.

Inside the box were the **Chaparral Objects**—items that were not, and could not be, present on Earth in 2119 or 2123, nor could they be present on December 31, 1999, when that same box appeared on the desk of the head of Chicago's Museum of Science and Industry, an event that changed our world in innumerable ways.

The first Chaparral Objects are:

s. 9: montage (embryos/animals)

Viable embryos of three extinct species—the ground sloth, the Quetzalcoatlus *northropi*, and the aurochs—along with plans to construct the equipment needed to revive, grow, and replicate the embryos. As you know, these species now flourish in the wild.

s. 10: still frame from *Lusitania*

A holographic video showing an overhead view of the sinking of the RMS *Lusitania* in 1915.

s. 11: still frame from Lascaux

Another holographic video showing a human couple from 17,000 years ago painting a section of cave wall in what would become France—two of the original artists of the famous Lascaux Cave.

s. 12: air sample w/ equipment

Labeled air samples from the time that each of the two holographic videos were taken—subsequent testing of CO2 and isotope levels confirmed that the air samples were indeed from those two eras.

For thirty years, on each December 31, a new box has appeared on that same desk in Chicago, a box containing new Operation Chaparral items from the future, along with video and photographs, some of which I will use in this presentation. The first box's contents were solely about proof of time travel, but the subsequent objects and knowledge from the future have been about saving us from ourselves. We no longer need proof that time travel is possible.

This is what everyone knows. This is what we teach our youth. These facts and events have become part of our history, albeit a history yet to come.

s. 13: Bostock and Nole at Pulitzer ceremony, 2127

The sudden and still-unexplained realization of time travel by Ms. Bostock, and the tireless efforts of her and Dr. Valerio Nole, have led to advances both now and in the future that far outstrip what would have been achieved during the normal— that is, unaffected by time travel—course of humanity. Of course, progress has been anything but smooth. I need not remind you of the setbacks—and tragedies—that even the wisest among us could not have foreseen.

s. 14: Indonesia uprising (triple crater, from space)

There will always be a vocal minority who wish that Ms. Bostock will never have had that flash of inspiration and had never sent proof of that inspiration back in time. But, overall, most of humanity agrees that time travel has been a boon to mankind, thanks to the new technologies that we have developed.

s. 15: UN flag

We have been brought together as a people, as a species, like never before.

s. 16: ISOPLEX reactor, Brazil

Energy is both nearly free and unlimited.

s. 17: restored wetlands, Louisiana

The air, the water, the Earth, are as clean and pure as they were thousands of years ago. So many of our past troubles and issues have been left to history.

Ladies and gentlemen, I need to tell you now that this is the part of my presentation where second grade is over.

s. 18: TRT symbol

I have been assured that the information I am about to share will remain strictly confidential. Thank you in advance for your cooperation.

Ladies and gentlemen, Emily Bostock was NOT the first to discover time travel.

`[pause for reaction]`

There have been others. Eighteen others. Some are dead. Some will be born in the future. Some will not be born at all. But all of them, alive or dead, born or not, independently discovered time travel and rewove the threads of Earth's past to the point that the original unaltered fabric is lost and meaningless.

Ladies and gentlemen, I am here today to tell you how I—we—know this. And I am here today to tell you that in three days, all of our progress, all of our peace, and all of our history, will be erased, replaced by an abomination, a twisting of our past so vast and so grotesque that there will remain no semblance to any of the familiar. And there is only one way to stop it.

s. 19: Questions/Break

I will now pause for questions.

LET LOOSE

In 2019, I saw a submission opportunity from anti*lang*, a creative writing hub that published online and print anthologies focusing on brevity and weirdness. This issue was looking for speculative fiction.

I had written plenty of short stories in the speculative space—science fiction, fantasy, and horror. The submission did stress that they embraced stories that played with form and structure, so I decided that if I was going to submit something, it would be fun to really push it.

I've always loved PowerPoint, Microsoft's presentation software. I used to teach the software back in my learning and development days. Was there a way to write something really weird that fused a speculative short story with PowerPoint?

Given that anti*lang* embraced out of the ordinary formatting (from what I saw in their previous issues), I could have formatted this in typical PowerPoint fashion with "slides," but I decided to go with more straightforward text and use different fonts to show the speaker notes, what was pictured on each slide, and the reminders to the speaker to pause, take questions, and such.

The speaker notes tell the story, the reminders for the speaker help to set the tone, and the descriptions of the slide images help the reader visualize what is going on. Hopefully, they combine to tell a story.

What made this story fun to write is that I let loose with the creativity with no plan to make any of what I put in here make sense. I don't know why I picked the *Lusitania*; I don't know why I chose those particular extinct species; I had no plan for tying in the Lascaux human cave painters to any of the other stuff. I didn't have to for this short story, because the story wasn't about making the science make sense outside of the story. It was about a scientist who was going to present a PowerPoint presentation that started off innocuous and ended terrifying (but still with time for questions).

It was fun to write without a plan (because I knew that no

plan was needed). Although I enjoy writing without a plan, it's hard to turn that part of my writing mind off. Here, I could use whatever nouns came to mind first (*Lusitania!* aurochs!) without trying to connect them. I didn't have to explain how time travel worked, because everyone in the story's audience would already know how time travel worked (but would still be baffled by the logic of it). As long as the reader could accept that time travel existed, I didn't need to do more.

In "Little Devils," I talked about playful writing—writing without consequences. "Chaparral" is like that but without boundaries on purpose.

Sometimes we writers should be as weird as we want and as weird as we can. If things don't make sense and it won't break the plot, let them make no sense. If you want to use a narrative form that isn't straight narrative text (maybe an Excel spreadsheet? maybe vertical text instead of horizontal text? maybe a recipe?) and you can still tell a solid story, go for it.

"Chaparral" worked (at least enough for anti*lang* to publish it) because for a short time, I ignored all the story barriers I might have usually thrown in front of myself—logic, why any of the story events happened, why those creatures, why those particular dates—and just wrote. I've used the term "bold" writing before in this book, and that is the sort of writing I love to see from my clients in their novels—the charge ahead, get out of my way, no holds barred writing. If it's too bold, it can be fixed later.

I love to see client writing that's too bold than not bold enough—it's also easier to edit. An editor's job is easier when we can work to lower someone's voice instead of getting them to speak up.

This is also a good way to write for fun, like I talked about in "Little Devils," except for that piece, it was all about ensuring that we write without fear of consequence. That applies here, too, but I like to take this approach for work that is going out in the world. It's much more common to get feedback from agents and editors that a writer "held back" than "was too bold." If you are submitting a short story like I did here, you probably aren't going to get praise that you "stuck to a traditional form" instead of "tried something too different." Our fear of making a mistake as writers can be overblown. And usually *is* overblown.

How our writing will appeal to our readers is really subjective, but if you have a choice between "give them what they've seen a billion times before" and "give them something they haven't seen before," I'd go with the latter. That doesn't always work—for example, if you are writing a cozy mystery or a sweet romance novel, or anything in genres where readers have strict expectations, you have to meet those expectations. You can still be creative, but a sweet romance means the couple gets together, not dies in quicksand and the book is formatted as PowerPoint slides.

And if you are submitting a novel or story to a place that has submission requirements, always follow those—if they say that they don't want experimental fiction, then they don't want experimental fiction. If they say they want 5,000-word stories, then they don't want a haiku.

But in most cases, if you want to write a short story, and you come to a crossroads with structure or form or plot or character, and you have free rein to choose, and the paths are "the same old same old" and "shockingly different," go for "shockingly different." That push might unleash a new side of your writing that you'll love.

Lesson learned: stories can succeed when you forget about all the reasons why they can't succeed.

DRAFT WIKI ARTICLE: THE ASTOUNDING RACE 45

Draft Wiki Article: The Astounding Race 45

(draft created December 8, 2034 by user <u>tarcameragal</u> (user rating 4.5, articles contributed: 89), 17:35:09 CST—autosaved)

The Astounding Race 45

- **Presented by:** Phil Keohane
- **Number of Teams:** 11
- **Winners:** GpY4tD and XpY4tM (unofficial—announced)
- **Distance Traveled:** approx. 31,000 miles (approx. 50,000 km)
- **Continents Visited:** 4
- **Countries Visited:** 10
- **Cities Visited:** 19
- **No. of Episodes:** 12 (11 produced, 1 shot, none aired)
- **Producing Network:** CBS in partnership with <u>CTV</u> (Canada)

- **Original Release:** Scheduled for February 15—May 3, 2035; season unaired
- **Filming Dates:** November 6—December 8, 2034

Intro

The Astounding Race 45 was the forty-fifth and final installment of the American reality television show *The Astounding Race*. It featured eleven teams of two, each with a pre-existing relationship, in a race around the world for prize money.

The season had been slated to premiere in the United States (CBS) and Canada (CTV) on February 15, 2035, with the two-hour finale scheduled for broadcast on May 3, 2035.

The Astounding Race Background

In *The Astounding Race*, teams of two compete against other teams in a race around the world. Each televised episode of the show focuses on one leg of the race. In each leg, teams typically fly or drive to a new city or country, compete against other teams to complete obstacles, and vie to finish that leg before other teams. The last team to complete each leg is eliminated from the race, although some legs are deemed to be "non-elimination" legs, in which the last-place team can stay in the race but is penalized in some fashion.

Production Development and Filming

This was the fifth season filmed with HoloDef 16K Drone cameras. Principal filming began on November 6, 2035 with host Phil Keohane kicking off the race in New Miami, Florida, the site of this season's starting line. This season marked the first time that a non-human team participated in the competition. The two production twists this season were that the winners were to receive $20 million, doubling the $10 million prize from the previous eight seasons, and that teams coming in last during any elimination leg (through leg 10) were forced to battle a Grindour Devourer with their bare hands and could stay in the competition if they defeated the beast. The latter rule change was a directive from the Grindour Alliance, which had threatened Earth with planet-wide immolation unless the Alliance could institute new *The Astounding Race* competition rules of its choosing (see "We Are Not Alone! Alien Fleet Materializes Above Greenland, Warns Earth Of Imminent Destruction Unless Certain Demands Met" and "They've Been Watching! You'll Never Guess What TV Show The Grindour Alliance Fell In Love With!").

This season marked the first time in the show's run that the first team to arrive at the finish line was not declared the official race winner. It was also the first season to be produced and filmed but not aired, and the first season in which contestants were eaten alive.

Cast

See also *List of The Astounding Race (American TV Series) Contestants*

Season 45 contestants included twin sisters and competitive cyclists Jean and Jill Philbrick, former child actors Dash McRory and Tim Dole, Grindour Alliance tourists GpY4tD and XpY4tM, and NFL teammates Oliver Sans and D'Angelo Hubbard.

Due to the Grindour threat of planet-wide immolation unless a Grindour team was allowed to compete in the show, the team of GpY4tD and XpY4tM took the place of a previously announced team, farmers Daniel "D.K." Keith and Tory Larue (see

"Grindour Alliance Tourists Demand Participation in CBS Reality Show *The Astounding Race*"). Daniel and Tory were promised slots on Season 46, which will not be produced.

Oliver and D'Angelo were originally cast for Season 43 but pulled out due to D'Angelo tearing an ACL during a pre-season game against the New York Metros. After Season 44 aired, CBS announced that Oliver and D'Angelo accepted an offer to be contestants in Season 45 (see "NFL Stars To Compete On *The Astounding Race*").

GpY4tD and XpY4tM were the first non-human team to compete in a season of *The Astounding Race.* They were also the first race participants to breathe sulfur trioxide, necessitating their use of SO3 tanks during the race, and the first team, due to their size, to be required to fly on cargo planes and be transported in tractor trailers rather than driving their own vehicles or taking commercial flights or hovertrains (see "Alien Giants Necessitate Changes To *TAR* Production: Source").

Dash McRory was the third TAR contestant to be a child of a previous contestant (joining Sarah Alms and Thomas McRory —see Season 22). See also *List of The Astounding Race (American TV Series) Contestants*.

Results Table

Team	Relationship	Position by Leg											
		1	2	3	4	5	6	7	8	9	10	11	12
GpY4tD & XpY4tM	Grindour Tourists	1	1	2	1	1	6	1	6	1	1	1	2
Terry & Cole	Holo Vloggers	9	4	9	3	6	4	4	2	2	3	3	1
Oliver & D'Angelo	NFL Players	4	2	4	5	5	5	3	4	5	2	2	3
Sharon & Bettina	Mother and Daughter	2	6	7	6	4	7	5	1	3	4	4	
Jean & Jill	Sisters/ Bicyclists	8	3	3	2	2	3	2	5	4	5		
Frank & Marlow	Dating Couple	5	8	8	8	3	1	6	3	6			
Brooke & Barbie	Street Artists	3	6	6	7	7	2	7					
Stefan & Fritz	Father and Son	10	9	1	4	8							
Dash & Tim	Former Actors	6	7	5	9								
Jie & Huiling	NASA Engineers	7	10										
Cam & J'Tal	Best Friends	11											

- blocks shaded in light gray indicate a team placing last in a leg but not eliminated due to the leg being deemed a non-elimination leg (legs 3, 6, 8)
- blocks shaded in dark gray indicate an eliminated team being forced to battle a Grindour Devourer with their bare hands to remain in the race, but each team was eaten alive by the Devourer and therefore remained eliminated (legs 1-2, 4-5, 7, 9-11)

Notes on Race Legs

Leg 3, 6, and 8 had been secretly deemed elimination legs before the start of the race but were changed to non-elimination legs due to the Grindour threat of planet-wide immolation if GpY4tD and XpY4tM did not place first in any leg. Legs 4, 7, and 9 were then deemed as elimination legs instead of a non-elimination legs, keeping GpY4tD and XpY4tM in the race.

In Leg 4, XpY4tM severed the tip of its tentacle as it attempted to complete a race task (rolling an oak barrel of <u>whiskey</u> along a narrow alley in <u>Slane, County Meath, Ireland</u>). XpY4tM's <u>acidic</u>

blood soaked several bystanders, killing two and injuring five. The team of GpY4tD and XpY4tM incurred a thirty-minute penalty but still came in first in the leg, four minutes ahead of second-place finishers Jean and Jill.

The medical team intervened again during the race. In Leg 7, two teams, dating couple Frank and Marlow and street artists Brooke and Barbie, raced to the finish mat and collided, causing both Frank and Barbie to suffer concussions. Barbie hit the ground first, but she and Brooke were eliminated due to Barbie not touching the mat after she fell.

In the eight elimination legs before the last leg, teams were forced to watch the eliminated team battle the Grindour Devourer. All of the remaining team members became violently ill when the Devourer ate the team members during these elimination battles, necessitating a brief shutdown of filming during and after each battle to quell hysteria.

In Leg 12, holographic vloggers Terry and Cole Shea arrived first at the finish line at the Gateway Arch in St. Louis, Missouri, but second-place finishers GpY4tD and XpY4tM were unofficially declared the winners of *The Astounding Race 45* due to the Grindour threat of planet-wide immolation should they not win. Terry and Cole refused to give up their earned first-place finish. After pleading unsuccessfully with Terry and Cole, host Phil Keohane then shut down filming. Various world leaders called Terry and Cole to try to convince them to give up their first-place finish to save the planet and humanity, but the team remained resolute that they were the race's true winners. Keohane then ordered filming to start back up and began to announce that GpY4tD and XpY4tM had been declared the official winners of the race over the protestations of Terry and

Cole, but before Keohane could finish, GpY4tD and XpY4tM transported to a Grindour destroyer, angry that Terry and Cole refused to relinquish their win. The Grindour fleet then initiated planet-wide immolation (see <u>"Breaking! Grindour Fleet Firing Huge Energy Weapons at Earth!"</u>), leading to the destruction of

WARP THE NORMAL

I've always been fascinated by the printed word. Those diner placemats with all the local ads? Love them! When I'm a tourist, I will always "read the plaque." At my bachelor party, my friends gifted me…a big box of their junk mail.

When I was twelve, we moved to a town that had a supermarket that gave out S&H Green Stamps with purchases. You saved up the stamps, put them in books, then you redeemed the books for items in a catalog. I loved reading that catalog, marking off all the items we'd eventually own (the stamps never really piled up the way I thought they would). I think that was my first foray into how words could be used for marketing. The catalog listed some towels, and I still remember the description: "soft cotton on one side, thirsty terry on the other!" Exciting!

I showed the description to my mom, eager to let her in on my discovery that the future of towel technology was here.

"It's a towel," she said. "That's how all towels are made."
Oh.

In "One House, Two Stories" and "Harry's Diner," I played with the traditional newspaper form by including points of view and inner thoughts that shouldn't be in a newspaper story. Here in "Draft Wiki Article," I wanted to take a common form of displaying information (a Wikipedia article) and fill it with fictional information.

It still had to tell a story, though, so I decided to recap the "current" season of *The Astounding Race*, a fictional version of the current TV series *The Amazing Race*, and have it written by someone on the show's production team (tarcameragal). She's furiously trying to keep her wiki article up to date while there is an alien invasion happening, to the point that the planet is getting immolated (a word I happened to like for this story—it just sounded right) as she's typing, and she never gets to finish her final sentence. Luckily her draft gets autosaved—perhaps the last article Earth ever has!

Now, this story will land with readers if they are a) familiar with Wikipedia and b) familiar with *The Amazing Race*. If they are familiar with just Wikipedia, they'll get that it's a fictional story because it's set in the future. If they know *The Amazing Race* but don't know anything about Wikipedia, they'll probably be able to follow along because I've constructed *The Astounding Race* just like *The Amazing Race*, but the story won't be as fun because the structure and format won't be familiar. If they don't know about Wikipedia or *The Amazing Race*, they'll probably think this story is a mess, and I won't blame them. The readers who are familiar with both might join them, and I won't blame them either. This was written more for me than for anyone else!

It's fun to take something familiar and warp it with the unfamiliar. Say you're at a diner, and they have those great placemats with the ads. You'll probably see ads for an insurance agent, and a roofer, and a landscaper, and maybe a real estate agent. But think about what else you could see? Or how you could rewrite those ads to make them either brutally honest or brutally false?

Look at all the fine print on the back of any bill you receive.

What are they really trying to say, and how could you rewrite that to make it funny or terrifying? Is there a story in there?

If you still get a physical newspaper (if not a daily, then a weekly or monthly free local one), go through a section and look at all the photographs. Could you rewrite all the captions so that the photographs taken together tell one story? That is a really fun challenge, by the way!

Could you tell a full story through a series of fake ads emulating those on Craigslist?

Or say there is something really mundane, like an appliance instruction manual. But two people at the factory slipped in some back and forth messages about their relationship. Or their thoughts about the working conditions at the factory. Or you totally warp the instructions for what the appliance does, turning the manual into something charming—or horrific.

The world has graced us with trillions of words in millions of formats and templates. We usually limit our stories to one format—the straight narrative, top to bottom, left to right, straight text. But our stories don't always have to fit into an easy template.

Lesson learned: not all stories have to be straight narratives.

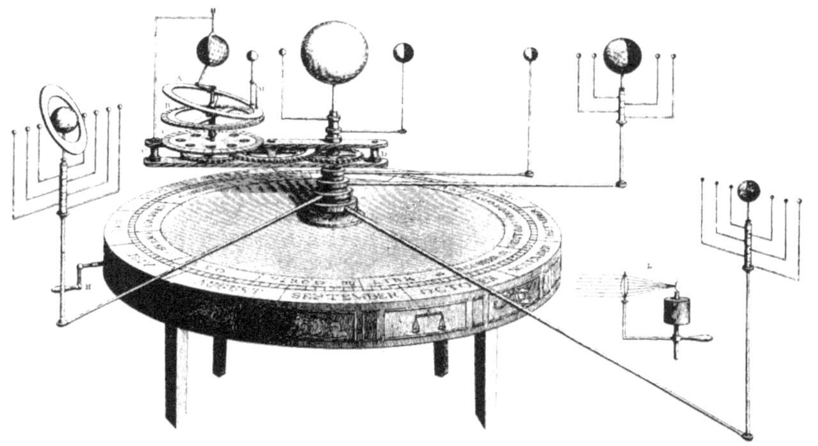

FREE MAN

The airman is one of dozens of men and women brought to a makeshift hospital after the latest enemy attack. They were trying to save Boston, but even as they fought, they knew it was futile.

A woman doctor walks over to the airman's cot, one of many set in a long row in a dark hallway of an abandoned shopping mall. The screams of injured patients fill the deserted corridors and echo off the long-closed storefronts.

Did they give you a shot for your pain when you came in, the doctor asks. The airman nods. Good, she says. The paste is still going to hurt, but it will neutralize the acid and prevent infection.

She looks closer at the scars on the airman's face. This isn't your first acid attack, is it, she asks. The airman shakes his head no.

The doctor cuts away the airman's shirt and uses a child's paintbrush to apply green paste from a glass bowl to his chest and neck. The paste smells like mustard and gasoline, as the airman knew it would. The doctor notices the airman squinting at the paintbrush as his eyes tear up from the pain and the smell.

It's the best we can do, she says, indicating the paintbrush. There aren't many supplies left.

She asks the airman his name. He tells her in a pained whisper, which is all he can manage because of the burns to his mouth and throat.

Do you have family in Boston, she asks. He shakes his head no.

She's silent for a bit, then says, mine were in Houston when they arrived.

The airman knows what happened in Houston. Everyone does. I'm so sorry, he mouths.

Now I keep getting pushed east, the doctor replies as she paints the airman's wounds with paste. East and north, like everyone else. Can't go much further east and north than Boston. I'm not even supposed to be doing this.

You're not a doctor? the airman manages to whisper, then adds, uh oh.

She stifles a laugh. I'm an OB/GYN, she says. A fertility specialist. Not that people need fertility specialists any longer. The enemy has taken care of that.

The airman doesn't reply. He doesn't need to.

They're running out of surgeons, you know, she continues. Even in Boston, the airman asks in a whisper. I thought Boston was loaded with surgeons. The doctor stifles another laugh. Even in Boston, she says.

Through the haze of the narcotic and the pain, the airman sees that the doctor has kind eyes. They're almond colored, one a little lower than the other, but in that charming way that he's always found attractive. She's wearing thick, red-framed glasses. He'd call her glasses quirky, if quirky was still a thing that mattered. She has a slightly crooked nose, freckles, and long auburn hair tied up in a bun. A few scars from acid burns dot her forehead and hands.

The doctor uses a comb to pick pieces of melted plastic from the airman's curly, black hair, then lifts a cup of water to his lips.

Before the aliens arrived, the airman wondered who he'd spend his life with. Everybody used to daydream, but there's no reason for anyone to do that now. The woman he imagined was much like this doctor. Striking, in that imperfect way. Caring. Smart. Quirky. He never imagined her having acid scars, but everyone has acid scars now. Acid scars, like daydreams, no longer matter.

The doctor finishes painting the airman's chest and neck with the green paste, then places a damp towel over his chest and a bandage on his neck. The airman wants to ask the doctor her name in return, but it's impossible for him to talk above a whisper, and even that hurts too much now. The doctor has a sticker on her maroon button-front sweater. Whatever name is written on the sticker is smeared with blood. The doctor moves to the next of the wounded, and the airman fades to sleep.

The doctor treats the airman many times over the next several days. She changes his dressings and applies more of the paste, and she talks to him even though he still can't talk above a whisper. She no longer wears the bloody sticker. He still wants to ask her name, but now it feels too late, as if he's missed his opportunity.

On the sixth night, the doctor starts to apply the paste, but then stops. She leans in and whispers, Boston's no longer safe. They're going to take you and the others by boat across the river and over to MIT. The buildings there have stronger sub-basements. It'll be safer. I'll be over once everyone is moved.

The doctor takes his hand, and the airman quivers at her touch. Her eyes are sad, but the airman sees something else in her eyes besides sadness. Save us when you're able, the doctor says to him. And if you can't save us, then save yourself. I'll see you across the river. If I don't find you, then you find me. She squeezes his hand, then lifts it and presses it to her lips. The airman's heart throbs.

After she finishes treating him, the doctor sits on the end of the airman's cot and writes in a blue notebook. It has a hand-drawn snake symbol on the cover. The airman would learn years later that the symbol is called a caduceus.

During the choppy trip across the river, the airman hears shouting, weapons fire, and the ever-present whine from enemy aircraft. He keeps his eyes closed as the boat runs dark on the black Charles River.

When the airman wakes up in the morning, much of Boston is gone. He spends two weeks in the new makeshift hospital in the sub-basement, but he never sees the woman doctor.

Once he can walk, the airman decides to search for the doctor in the remains of Boston, but before he can leave the makeshift hospital, there is a surrender. The airman, along with many others, is taken to an enemy factory. He thinks that the factory is in Rhode Island, but nothing looks the same now, so it's hard to say. An enemy amputates the airman's right foot to keep him from running away. You'll get used to it, the other enslaved men and women say. One foot for the pedal, two hands for the levers.

Nine years pass. The airman thinks of the doctor every day as he toils for the enemy. He thinks of how her lips felt on his hand. That memory keeps him sane. When the airman is too weak to work in the factory any longer, the enemy tells him, in their way, that he is now a Free Man. They give the airman an artificial foot to replace the one that they amputated.

The airman hears that some of the people who made it out of Boston nine years ago ended up in Buffalo. He decides to walk to Buffalo. There is no longer any way to get to Buffalo, or anywhere else, except by foot.

The airman walks slowly at first because he's not used to his artificial foot. There is plenty of water around because the enemy likes things warm and moist. The airman occasionally travels with small groups of people, most of whom also have artificial feet, but most of the time he walks alone. At night, he lights a fire, when he can find dry tinder, and stares at the sky. He wonders if the doctor is looking at the same sky. The night sky is filled with stars that he could not see before the enemy arrived. The night sky is also filled with enemy aircraft.

The airman thinks about the doctor during his walk to Buffalo. He wonders what her name is. He settles on Eve, in part because he has always liked that name, and in part because Eve was the first woman. Perhaps that was what was written on the sticker on her sweater. Eve. The airman considers other names, like Darlene or Jessie, but to him, she didn't look like a Darlene or Jessie. To him, she looked like an Eve.

The airman imagines what a life with Eve would be like— laughing, surrounded by children, going on picnics, going to ballgames. But there are no more ballgames, and no more children, and very little laughter.

The walk from Rhode Island to Buffalo takes the airman forty-three days. When he arrives in Buffalo, the airman asks where the doctors are. Try the Central Terminal, some people say. The airman finds the Central Terminal building. The office tower is destroyed, the rubble strewn on the surrounding streets, but part of the lower building is still intact.

The airman finds some doctors, but not the woman doctor. One of the doctors, a harried older man covered with acid scars, says that a group of doctors branched off to Toronto years ago. He thinks that some of them may have come from Boston, but there's no way to know.

Do you know how to get to Toronto, the airman asks the harried doctor.

Keep Lake Ontario on your right, the doctor says.

The walk from Buffalo to Toronto takes the airman eight days. In Toronto, the people point him to the Robarts Library. It's a massive building, and it appears untouched by enemy attack. Inside, the airman finds a pleasant woman at the first-floor reception desk. The entry is illuminated by torches. The woman looks up from her book and asks, can I help you, acting for all the world as if she's worked at this library forever and no alien invasion is going to change that. The airman says, I'm looking for a doctor. I don't know her name. She was working in Boston before the surrender nine years ago.

I don't ask people where they are from, as it's none of my business, the pleasant woman replies, but feel free to look on the fifth floor. That's where the doctors sleep. Take the stairs to five, then look for the sign that says Maps. The woman returns to her book.

The airman says thank you and takes the stairs to the fifth floor. The maps room is deserted, and the maps are gone. The airman finds an area full of cots, the original shelving shoved against one wall, then spots several desks, each piled high with personal belongings.

A worn and filthy maroon sweater is draped over a chair in front of one of the desks. Among the few personal items on the desk is a notebook, its blue cover bent and beaten, the hand-drawn caduceus faded with time.

The airman sits in the chair, puts his head in his hands, and sobs.

Later, he hears sharp footsteps. He looks up. The woman doctor halts when she sees the airman sitting at her desk. Her eyes grow wide, and her mouth opens in shock.

The airman stands unsteadily. I saved myself, he says, his

voice trembling, his thick, curly, black hair now nearly gray. I couldn't save you, but I saved myself, like you asked.

The doctor shrieks the airman's name, then runs to him, laughing, her arms outstretched. Before she reaches him, the airman realizes that it doesn't matter what her real name is. To him, she will always be his Eve.

FIND THE BEST VERSION

This story started as a draft synopsis for a novel-length work. I had added in some description of the aliens and some middle scenes to give myself something to work with later. A draft synopsis, maybe an 800-word high-level summary of a novel, beginning to end, is one way to know if there's enough story to carry through to a novel before you actually start writing it. Later, you can expand the synopsis into an outline, giving it some structure, like acts and chapters and scenes.

I was set to start outlining the book, but I wanted to be sure that I had the core of a solid story, so I looked more closely at that synopsis.

I did nail the "spine" of the story in that synopsis—the airman's brief memories of the doctor were the one thing that had kept him sane through years of horror, and he needed to find her. It's not that he loved her—it's that he needed to know that she was safe, I think. The same for her—she didn't love him, she may not have even thought of him, but she remembered him, and it seemed that not a lot of joy was left in their world, so maybe that reunion could be a happy ending.

Interesting. So I pared everything else from the synopsis and focused just on that storyline to see what it looked like apart from everything else. All of the other story elements like the aliens and battle scenes were begging me to put them back in—I still do think there could be a novel-length story here—but I focused on just the airman's search for the doctor, condensing all those years into less than 2,000 words and giving the airman and the doctor the happy ending in a still-hellish world.

Experienced writers come up with ideas all the time. Ideas are cheap. Ideas are plentiful. Ideas that could be turned into decent books (if we put in the work) are all around us. That doesn't mean that all those ideas need to be books.

Maybe they need to be combined into plot elements for one book. Maybe, like here, they can be short stories. Maybe they're best destined for a TV script or a song lyric. Maybe they're the plot of a novel one of your characters is working on (the book within a book!). Or maybe you can pass the idea off to another writer friend.

I like the idea of knowing when to stop—of turning what you think might be a novel idea into a novella or short story. For one, short stories are faster to write. Second, once the short story is written, that idea won't keep nagging you to do something with it (and you can always expand it later). As I've talked about earlier, writing outside of our book projects is both fun and needed, so why not use some of these ideas?

Also, if you like the idea of pitching your stories to "Hollywood," meaning production companies: short stories are great ways to pitch movie ideas. Usually that means short stories of 5,000 to 10,000 words, not like the much shorter stories I have here. But those stories are long enough to tell a movie-length story; they solidify your idea as your intellectual property published; they're easier to summarize than a novel; and they can be expanded into a novel. The odds are low, of course, for any of our short stories or novels to be picked up and adapted and produced, but just know that short stories do have their place, and that if you dream of seeing your work on the big screen, your work does NOT have to be a novel for that to happen.

Less-experienced writers often treat ideas as precious commodities, things that come along just a few times in a lifetime, things that need to be treated as so delicate that we can't risk even handling them without fear of destroying them.

Nope. Ideas are resilient. They aren't gossamer creations; they can be vague at first, but then they are more like clay, meant to be shaped, formed, torn down, combined, and built back up into something strong.

If an idea sounds like a book, maybe it is a book. But maybe it's a short story. Maybe it's destined for another writer. Maybe it's meant for the trash (although I keep almost all ideas in a notes app, except for the really bad ones).

But whatever you do with it, do *something* with it. Don't treat it like it will be the only idea you will ever have. Don't stop coming up with new ideas just because you have one idea. I am willing to bet, and I don't even know you, that with any successful television series you are watching now, the creator of that series didn't have that one idea and then simply stopped having ideas because of that series idea. That idea may have come years before the show even started production.

As creators, it's not only our job to continually create, it's our passion.

Lesson learned: sometimes the best version of a story is not the one you set out to create.

DEATH TAKES A HALLIDAY

"You'll do great," Emily Halliday says as she straightens her husband Paul's tie. "You know what they say: if they bring you in for a third interview, then the job's already yours."

"I hope so," Paul replies. "I've been out of work for too long."

Emily frowns. "Turn around."

Paul turns. "What is it?"

"Your shirt is all wrinkled in the back."

"I'll leave my suit jacket on."

"Too formal," Emily says. "You're going to be there all day. Iron your shirt again. I'll drop the kids off at preschool and hit the grocery store. I'll be back before you leave. Kids, say good luck to Daddy."

"Good luck, Daddy!" Brayden and Angelina, the twins, pound past Paul to grab their school backpacks.

Paul says his goodbyes, then heads upstairs to brush his teeth. He decides to wear his suit jacket during the entire interview. Better to overdress, he thinks, plus he hates ironing.

An otherworldly blue flash fills the bathroom and hallway,

followed by a loud pop coming from downstairs. Paul groans. Probably another CFL bulb in the kitchen biting the dust. Twenty-year lifespan, my ass. He heads for the stairs.

Halfway down, Paul catches a whiff of something horrible. It smells like low tide. Don't let it be the hermit crab, he thinks. Brayden is going to lose it if another hermit crab dies. He decides to check the bulb before checking on the hermit crab.

Paul continues down the stairs and into the living room, where he stops cold.

A towering figure floats above the carpet and nearly brushes against the ceiling. The figure wears a long, black cape but has no discernible body—Paul can see neither arms nor legs. The smell wafting from the figure is overpowering, a mix of sulfur and rotted fish. A deep hood covers the black hole where the figure's face should be.

"I am Death, Peter Halliday," the figure says in a gravelly voice. "You will soon die—"

"But I'm not Peter Halliday!" Paul stammers. "I'm *Paul* Halliday!"

"Oh. Hold on," Death says. It fishes in a pocket and brings out what looks to Paul like a smartphone, the device hovering in front of the cape as if held by an invisible hand. "You're right. *Paul* Halliday. Sorry. It's been a long day already." Death pockets the phone and starts again. "I am Death, Paul Halliday. You will soon die. I am here to—"

Paul screams. He turns and runs through the living room and into the dining room, where he stops. Death stands in front of him, blocking his path.

Paul continues to scream as he backs away from Death. The sleeve of Death's cape extends impossibly long toward Paul. When he hits the far wall, Paul puts his hands over his face and continues screaming until he feels something icy press against his chest. Then he is filled with a curious calm. His panic drains away, and he stops screaming. He takes his hands away from his face and sees Death's sleeve retreating.

"What did you just do to me?" Paul asks. "I feel empty. Am I dead?"

"Of course not," Death says. "Well, not yet. I got rid of your emotions, is all. That screaming was giving me a headache. You need to focus, Paul. We have work to do. And we don't have much time."

Before Paul can ask what Death means, a dog charges around the corner and stops before Death, wagging its tail.

"Well, well. Who's this little charmer?" Death asks.

"That's Roscoe," Paul says. "Are you going to kill him?"

"Please," Death said. "I don't kill. Plus, I'm a dog person." It bends down in front of the dog, a bull terrier. "Can you do tricks? How about paw?"

Roscoe waves his paw at Death. "Good boy," Death says. Then Death and Roscoe both turn to face Paul and wait.

"What?" Paul asks after a moment.

"Roscoe wants a cookie," Death says. "He did paw."

Paul goes into the kitchen to get Roscoe a cookie. Death follows, and it and Paul sat.

"Let me start from the top," Death says. "I am Death, Paul Halliday. You will soon die. I am here to make things easier for your loved ones."

Paul begins peppering Death with questions, which Death answers curtly.

When am I going to die? In twenty minutes.

How am I going to die? You will have a ruptured cerebral aneurysm.

How do you know that I'm going to die? You're on my list.

Will I feel anything? I don't know.

What will happen when I die? I will collect your soul.

Will Emily see you? I will leave before she returns.

Then comes the pleading. *I'm too young to die. My wife will be devastated. My kids will forget me. I have an interview this morning. There must be something you can do. There must be a way to change this. I don't want to die.*

Death is unprepared for the barrage of questions and pleading. It has assumed that Paul will act much more efficiently without his emotions.

"Look, Paul," Death interrupts. "You're going to die in"—it checks its phone again—"thirteen minutes. You can't change that. I can't change that. I show up after each death to collect the soul. That's my job. I don't talk to live people. I'm never seen by live people. That's the way it's always been done, anyway. At least, before today. But see, there's this new program."

"I don't understand," Paul says.

"It's what I was trying to say earlier. I'm here to make things easier for your loved ones."

"How can my death be easy on my loved ones at all?"

"It's like this," Death explains. "My higher-ups are displeased with the growing duplicity in the world. More and more, people keep secrets from those that they love. When they die, their loved ones find out about those secrets, and their lives can be ruined. All this lying and secret-keeping has upset The Balance. So my higher-ups"—at this, Death points an invisible arm up—"asked me to test out a new program. I have to start giving people the chance to get rid of their secrets before they die. This will supposedly make things easier on their loved ones and will start to restore The Balance. That's the goal, anyway."

"I see," Paul says.

"Things were fine the way they were, if you ask me," Death grumbles. "I've never cared about The Balance. That's above my pay grade. I do what I'm told, but I'm not happy about this new program. Not that I can be happy or unhappy, you understand. I don't have emotions myself. That's just an expression I use."

"Does the program work?" Paul asks. "Does it restore The Balance?"

"You're the first person in the new program," Death admits. "It's in the beta process. I chose you because you're home, you're alone, and you're perfectly healthy—for a few more minutes, anyway. All of that should make it easy for you to get rid of any secrets you have in the house. At least, I think it should. We'll see how it goes."

"How do I get rid of my secrets?" Paul asks.

"I haven't yet memorized what I'm supposed to say," Death says. It looked at its phone. "I'm going to read this straight from the script: what objects would you not want your family to find? What would you not want them to find out about you?"

Paul thinks for a moment. "Okay. I can think of a few objects, at least."

"Please collect them. And hurry," Death says. "You don't have much time."

Death sits while Paul scurries about the house. It stands when Paul returns with a box.

"Let's see what you've got," Death says, poking around in the box. "VHS tapes. Pills. And what are these?"

"They're driver's licenses. I stole them out of wallets and purses at my previous job. I don't know why I started doing it, but once I started, I couldn't stop. I was addicted to the thrill of it. They never caught me, but they suspected, so they used it as an excuse to get rid of me. I told Emily that I was laid off. I couldn't find a new job. Then I started using drugs."

"What about the VHS tapes?"

"I have these urges that would drive Emily away if she found out about them. I haven't looked at those tapes in years. I just can't bring myself to get rid of the tapes. I've always been broken. I keep so much from Emily. I keep so much from everyone. I am not a good person." Paul frowns. "It's funny. I constantly felt guilty and scared because of who I was and how much I hid, and what would happen if Emily found out about my secrets. Now I don't feel anything. I should be petrified—I'm about to die. But I feel at peace somehow, like I don't need any of that"—he gestures at the box—"any longer. It's like you're my confessor."

"Whatever," Death says. "Put the box on the floor."

Paul places the box on the floor and steps back.

Death extends a sleeve. There is a bright blue flash, and the box disappears.

"Well, that's that," Death says. "Those secrets are gone. Is there anything else you need to get rid of?" It pulls out the phone again. "Let me look at the checklist. Incriminating browser history? Compromising pictures? Salacious texts? Bodies in the basement? I'm kidding about that last one. I'd know about any bodies in the basement, of course."

"No," Paul says, "nothing like that. Wait, what about passwords?"

"Getting rid of passwords isn't on the list," Death says, checking its phone.

"Not getting rid of the passwords," Paul replies. "Writing down the passwords. Emily doesn't know some of my passwords. It will make things easier for her."

"Hmm." Death taps its invisible chin with an invisible finger. "The world is so complex nowadays. So digital. Things were much simpler when people spent their days sowing the fields or working the looms. No one worried about passwords or browser histories. Well, I suppose that writing down passwords is okay. I can see how that could make things easier on Emily. Like I said, this *is* a new program."

"Where should I put the passwords? Under the keyboard?"

"That's the first place everyone looks," Death said. "Emily would have seen them there already. It would look suspicious. Pick someplace where she hasn't looked but she'll find easily."

"My wallet. She never looks in there." Paul goes upstairs to retrieve his wallet from his suit jacket. When he returns, he takes a Post-It note, writes down some passwords, then quickly folds the paper and shoves it in his wallet.

"Not so fast," Death says. "Give me the note."

"Why?"

"You know why."

Paul sighs, then hands over the note, which has the passwords plus a line that reads, *Emily, I love you and the kids so much. Goodbye. Paul xoxo.*

"Nice try," Death says, crumpling the note and dropping it in its cape pocket. "Passwords only. Emily can't know that you knew you were going to die."

Paul writes a new note, shows it to Death, who approves it, and puts the note in his wallet, then places the wallet on the kitchen counter.

"You have two minutes left," Death says. "Where do you want to be when you die?"

"I guess the couch," Paul says, sounding resigned. "It's comfy."

They walk to the living room, and Paul sits on the couch. "I want to cry," Paul says. "I want to grieve. I want to be afraid. I want to feel something. *Anything.* But you stole my emotions. I feel like I'm already dead."

Roscoe hops on the couch and puts his head on Paul's lap. "Take care of Mommy and Brayden and Angelina, okay?" Paul says, patting the dog.

Death and Paul sit in unemotional silence until Paul tips forward, falling off the couch onto the floor and startling Roscoe, who runs out of the room.

Death collects Paul's soul, then thinks about Paul's last words: *You stole my emotions. I feel like I'm already dead.*

What is it like to have an emotion? Death will never know. But it thinks that it will need to understand emotions better if it is going to be forced to work with live people in this new program.

Death walks to the kitchen. It takes the note out of Paul's wallet, finds a pen, adds a crudely drawn heart to the note, and puts the note back in the wallet. It gazes out the window and thinks about emotions until it sees Emily's car pull into the driveway, then, with a flash of blue light, it disappears.

IDEAS ARE EVERYWHERE

Several years ago, I had this nagging thought: what if there was a way to have an hour of lead time before you died? What would you do with that lead time? Was an hour too much? What if you weren't home?

It wasn't a story idea, but more of a life idea. The thought would come and go at random times. Mostly it would pop up when I was at my (seldom-used) workbench in the basement, because that was where I was when I first had the idea. It actually got pretty annoying, because I used the workbench more to pile stuff on, and every time I piled stuff on the workbench, the idea came back into my head.

Finally, I had another idea: write a story about that idea to get it out of my head. And "Death Takes A Halliday" was born.

It worked! Now I sometimes think of an emotionless cloaked figure when I'm piling stuff on the workbench, but I no longer dwell on the question of what I'd do with an hour of lead time.

This is the thing with writers: we don't have to try too hard to find ideas—the ideas find us. And they don't always come as story ideas; they come as hounding thoughts. We just get in the way and don't see them as story ideas.

Sometimes they do come as snippets from a dream. Sometimes they come from overhead dialogue. Sometimes they come out of nowhere.

My first novel, *The Matildas*, was about a tiny publishing company that had a portal in its basement leading to a parallel Earth, and they took novels from one Earth and published them on their own Earth (essentially, they were book thieves). That idea came to me about fifteen years ago when I was mowing the lawn. I thought that would be the main plot, but it ended up only being the setting for a different mystery that could only take place with the parallel Earths. I've had plenty of ideas that came to me while I was mowing the lawn or doing other mundane work where I didn't need to be doing a lot of high-level thinking. I forget most of them before I can write them down, but that one stuck around long enough for me do something with it.

Other ones, like the one for this story, are uninvited guests—I don't need to write them down because they won't leave me alone. I've learned that it's best to either write a story with them or at least put them in my notes app with my story ideas or they'll continue to haunt me.

Most story ideas go nowhere, because most ideas aren't very good ideas. But if you don't embrace the idea of having a LOT of ideas, you won't have many good ideas, and even fewer ideas that turn into solid stories.

I've had writers ask me, "How do you come up with so many ideas? I only have one!" I can't tell them that they are wrong, but I think that maybe we are thinking about "idea" differently. I'd love to think that "idea" means something fully fleshed out, with complex characters and a unique plot and setting, ready for me to open a fresh Word document, the only work left being me typing 300,000 characters that don't need editing.

Nope. The idea is just the start. The idea might be five words. It's probably not a story, more of a "thing." For the book I mentioned, it was a portal in a basement that led to a parallel Earth. Then it was what they could do with it. I chose books because I'm a writer and it sounded fun. Then I had to set some rules (the portal broke all technology, so they couldn't bring across computers or whatever).

At that point, there was still no story. So if I ran into a literary agent and told them about my "book idea," they'd brush me off, because there WAS no book idea. There was just a (possibly) interesting conceit. There were no characters and no plot.

Having characters bring books back and forth between two Earths and publishing them as their own is kinda cool, but that's not really a story if it always works. There's no danger. Everything's normal.

Crime fiction writer Jim Thompson is quoted as saying, "There is only one plot—things are not as they seem." He was right.

In this story, it wouldn't be much of a story if Death was collecting souls like it normally did. That's where my nagging idea came in: Death has to deal with a new program, one where humans who were about to die had some lead time. Death is not a fan of this new program. Things are not as they seem, because Paul sees Death, and Death interacts with a live human, and together they work out some kinks with the new program, and Death considers emotions for the first time.

In the notes for "Free Man," I wrote about not treating ideas as precious. A writer's problem is usually the opposite. It's that we have so many ideas we'll never get to. Most of them aren't going to make it to the "this will make a fantastic book!" level. Some will get combined with other ideas to make a short story. I'm currently working on a long-term project with characters that I created for a project that went nowhere. The idea was okay, but the characters were better than the idea. The problem was that the characters also felt like they were in the wrong project. Then I had a new idea but I had no characters for it. I took the characters from the old project—that was a more serious mystery, and the new project is more comedy—and the characters fit perfectly. That happens a lot in writing. Many of our ideas are vague, but we know that there is something there; we just don't know what the "there" is yet.

As a freelance editor, I work with many new writers who are afraid that any outside person is going to steal their ideas. I guess it could happen, although I've never heard of an editor stealing anyone's ideas. The thing is, writers and editors have too many of our own ideas that we'll never get too—we'll *never* get to anyone else's ideas.

Although I'm always amazed at every client's imagination and world-building and characters and all that, I never want to write *their* ideas—I want to write *my* ideas. Being amazed at someone else's ideas isn't the same as being excited about writing those ideas.

I want to write the ideas begging to get out of my head and the ones filling up my notes app. That's where all these stories came from—an idea I had. I worked on them, I learned from them, and I became a better writer from them.

The only way to become a better writer is to write and read. In my opinion, there really is no such thing as writer's block—instead, there is writing and not writing, there is wanting to write and not wanting to write, there is being afraid to write and not being afraid to write. No other profession has a "block." Does your plumber not work one day because she has plumber's block? Does your lawyer fail to show up to represent you in court because they're blocked and can't come up with an argument to save you from going to jail?

All writers have the same tools—a blank page, a set of characters that can be combined into words, a set of rules about how those words go together, and an imagination. What sets productive writers apart is that they don't give up, they aren't afraid to try new things, they write even when they don't feel like writing, and they write because they can't NOT write.

I never tell my clients that they "must" write every day, or that they should write a certain amount of words every day, or that they won't have bad writing days. Writing is one of the easiest things in the world to NOT do when you don't feel like doing it. But it's on those days, the days when we don't feel like writing but we do it anyway, that we really do become "real" writers, then we marvel at what exits our heads.

Lesson learned: ideas are everywhere.

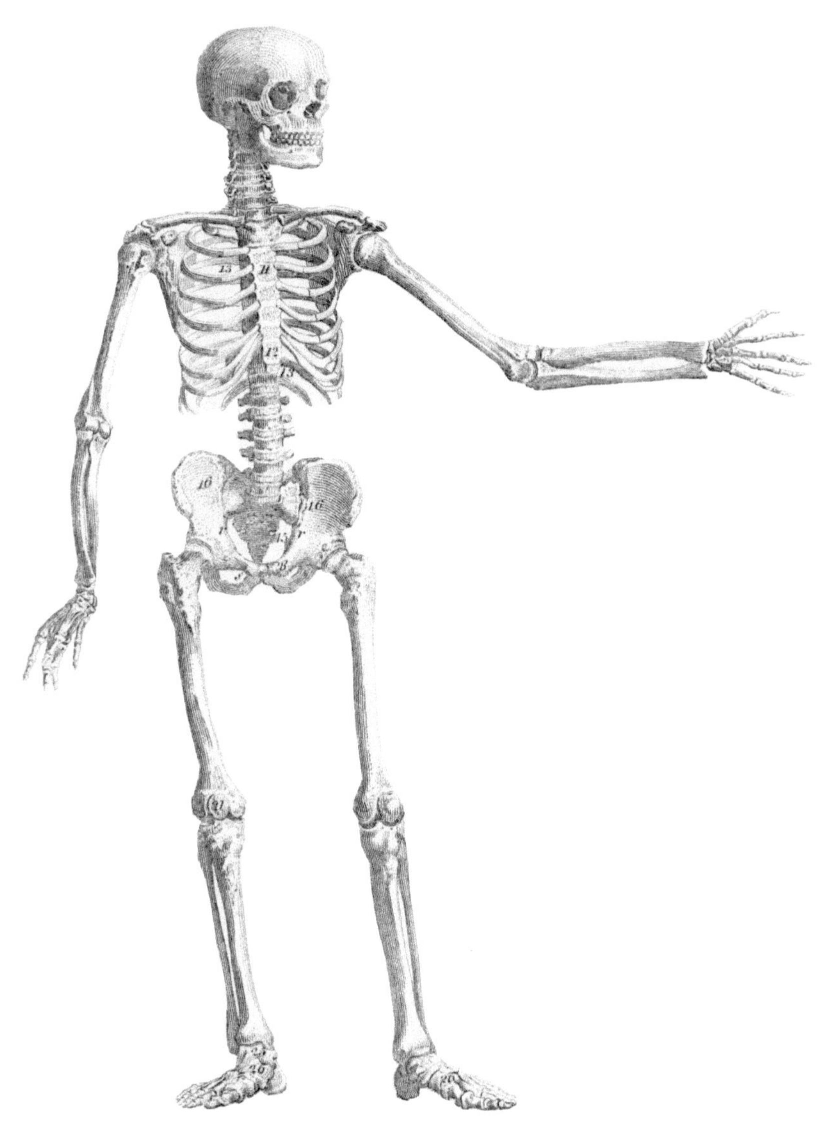

FEEDBACK!

Love a story? Hate a story? Have questions or thoughts about any of the "stories behind the stories" or about writing in general? Feel free to contact me by scanning the QR code below or sending me an email at:

exitaheadbook@gmail.com

I will reply individually!

ABOUT THE AUTHOR

Dave Pasquantonio is a freelance writer, book editor, and author living in Massachusetts. He's also an editor and story creator for Sterling & Stone, a multimedia story studio and publisher in Austin, Texas. His short fiction has been published in numerous anthologies and online and print journals, and he's written hundreds of newspaper columns and features. His first novel, *The Matildas*, a quirky sci-fi mystery about books, true love, and a parallel Earth, was published in 2020. His next novel, *Wicked Fun*, the first in a series about Jane Hawkins, an "unretired" serial killer, was published in May 2025.

Dave doesn't really do social media. He's already got too many things exiting his head. But you can learn more about him by visiting his website at:

www.davepasquantonio.com

www.ingramcontent.com/pod-product-compliance
Lightning Source LLC
Chambersburg PA
CBHW060543190726
48283CB00003B/849